MW01245180

Eye of the Eagle

Eye of the Eagle

Eric J. Collenette

Walker and Company
New York

Published in the United States of America in 1988 by the
Walker Publishing Company, Inc.

Library of Congress Cataloging-in-Publication Data

Collenette, Eric J.
    Eye of the eagle.

    Reprint. Originally published: London : Kimber,
1986.
    1. World War, 1939-1945--Fiction. I. Title.
PR6053.04236E9 1988   823'.914   88-74
ISBN 0-8027-1034-4

Printed in the United States of America

10 9 8 7 6 5 4 3 2 1

What passing-bells for these who die as cattle?
Only the monstrous anger of the guns.
WILFRED OWEN 1893-1918

One

Leading Seaman Seth Mortimer – Mort to his mates – watches the shuffling queue of disconsolate men collecting kit from the open hatch of the slop-room. They are wearing an ill-fitting assortment of clothing supplied by the rescue ship that hauled them out of the biting cold water of the Thames Estuary. Most of them are young, and the three-hour journey from the dockside to the scene of the disaster is their total experience of life at sea.

The tannoy of the newly refitted destroyer had called them to 'Stations for leaving harbour' before sun-up, and the older hands cursed their fumbling efforts as all ties were severed with the shore, and the last hawser slipped inboard through the fairlead to be reeled up on its drum.

Shaking free of the restrictions of the dockyard, she cleaved through the murky water of the ancient river towards the estuary and the open sea. She was at action stations, with damage control at first degree, and every hatch and door closed as she moved out of the close confines of the river into the bleak expanse of the roadstead that stretched out into the grey haze on either side. It was a sullen, mysterious wilderness of broken water that seemed to move with them as revolutions increased and her sleek stem threw aside hissing bow-waves to spread two folds of swell that licked the sleeping banks and rudely awakened the idle river boats so that they bucked and reared indignantly in their stagnant pools.

To some the first queasy warnings came as she shuddered and lifted to the influence of the encroaching sea, and they strove to hide their apprehension. Like their ship they were untried and untested; requiring many exercises and drills before being allowed out on their own. So two other destroyers ranged abeam to escort her through the swept channels to Harwich. Also in company, a smart cross-channel packet converted into a rescue ship took advantage of the small convoy as she steamed out to join a much larger group of ships plodding up the east coast. The cruel wind followed them out as though it enjoyed pushing them into the treacherous reaches, where the enemy was at his worst.

Lying on the seabed a sophisticated piece of scientific engineering waited for them, and its sensitive antenna stirred into life as the first vibrations from the approaching propellers reached it. The trigger mechanism came alive to prime itself ready from the precise moment to detonate 1,000 kilos of high explosive, and it worked perfectly. The destroyer reeled to the violent eruption beneath her keel. It broke her spine and ruptured the thin, steel plates to allow the sea to invade her boiler-room. In moments she began to roll over, and her crew fought desperately to get clear, launching themselves into the dark water where they struggled against her pull until the strong hands of rescuers plucked them out and into the warm comfort of the rescue ship.

Less than one fifth of her company survived, and now they stand in motley attire waiting to be kitted out once more, supervised by Mort, who guides them through with his blunt words and unvarnished manner. Routine forces them back to reality, overcoming the shock and residual fear that makes the very thought of going back to sea unbearable. They have lost everything: their personal gear, their kit, and most of all their spirit, but the Navy has the machinery to rebuild their confidence, and ensure that the money spent training them to be sailors is not wasted, for there are other ships hungry for crews, and at this crucial time in the war even the short spell of survivors' leave they will get is ill-afforded. Mort is part of that machinery and knows better than to allow his feelings to show.

The industrious little Wren issuing the slops has no time for such contemplations. Her duty is to replace uniforms with due regard for the correct procedure laid down to ensure that there is no undue wastage in these times of austerity. In cold tones she checks off the items to each man while Mort stands by, watching her carefully and concealing his compassion beneath a gruff exterior.

'Two pairs socks – two pairs underpants – two ves – ' she hesitates, glancing up at the bedraggled remains of a vest; all that is left of the seaman's kit. 'Oh no,' she states firmly, congratulating herself on saving the Admiralty two shillings and sixpence, 'one vest – two whi – '

'Hang about!' protests Mort, and, with his hand against the seaman's chest, grasps a fistful of decomposing vest and rips it clear of the man, whose expression is unchanging as he stands between the pert little Wren and the belligerent leading hand while they glare at each other. 'Two vests,' growls Mort with a threatening look.

Reluctantly she places a second garment on the pile and the numbed sailor accepts his due without a word. The cold has not thawed from his aching bones, nor the shock from his mind, so he needs to be urged on with a gentle prod to send him out into the sunshine.

*

Later, with the memory of those dead-eyed men still fresh in his mind, Mort makes his way back to the mess-deck where working parties are returning to clean up in time for dinner. He is new to the routine of life in barracks, and content to fall in with the scheme of things. Portsmouth Barracks is old, providing temporary accommodation for a continual stream of men who are between ships, so the amenities are spartan. There are no lockers, only racks ranged down the length of the bare dormitory to hold kit-bags, while the hammock nettings overflow with canvas cocoons, bulging with the extra gear stuffed in with the blanket and bedding issued to each man. The long, cavernous habitat is punctuated at intervals with iron stoves to provide heating for the messes, which consist of nothing but plain wooden tables and stools, too meagre for the overcrowded conditions of a wartime navy.

There is the minimum of supervision and organisation, for the main purpose of it all is to move men in and out as quickly as possible. In these circumstances the situation is wide open to petty criminals with crafty brains and no sense of purpose other than their own gratification. The influx of green 'Hostilities Only' conscripts from a multitude of backgrounds has swelled until they vastly outnumber the regular seamen who would have behaved with self-discipline cultivated by years of service. Instead, a regime of 'every man for himself' prevails, and some messdecks are turned into jungles, where to survive a man must be more wily than his neighbour.

Mort arrives as the rum is being issued by the leading hand of the mess. Until now there has been no time to get to know other members of his temporary billet, and even now he lines up with little interest in anything other than the welcome tot of grog. The man who ladles out the strong mixture has close-cropped hair thatching a lean, heavily-lined face, pockmarked and ravaged by brutality inherited from generations of ancestors to whom roguery is a way of life. Somehow this villain has discovered a way to manipulate the system and avoids the daily draft-lists that would inflict him unto the messdecks of sea-going ships. So, left to their own devices, he and his cronies have established a protection racket in their mess, but have sense enough to steer well clear of the likes of Mort who would have rumbled their little game.

The man's name is Malloy, and he glares up into Mort's face for a second or so before meticulously measuring out a tot. It is the custom for a new member of the mess to offer 'sippers' when he draws his first issue, but Mort pointedly declines when he sees the expression on the other man's features. There is malice in the narrow eyes, and a contemptuous twist to his mouth. The way Malloy and his band of hangers-on go about things fills Mort with suspicion. He takes his rum to the far end of the table, away from the iron stoves where most men gather to drink their tots. There he sits watching the ritual carefully, and what he sees confirms his suspicions.

Recruits arriving fresh from training establishments try to come to grips with their strange new environment, and prove easy victims for Malloy, who descends on them like a vulture. They warm to his smile of welcome, and those who are old enough to draw rum donate liberal offerings in their anxiety to curry favour, and it is tipped back into the rum fanny by the benign leading hand as though it is his divine right. Mort grins knowingly: he's seen it all before. Sod the stupid young bastards! They will have to learn the hard way, like he did.

As he watches, a further ritual takes place. A new man enters the mess to produce his joining-routine form. The cut of his uniform shows he is fresh out of training school, and he is taken aside by one of the henchmen where a short argument ensues, during which the nervous protests of the newcomer are overwhelmed by a concerted verbal attack from Malloy's men as they crowd round. It is clear that they do not like his responses, and when he walks away indignantly to stow his kit-bag in the racks it is promptly seized by one of the gang and transferred to another place. Mort notices that there is a distinct dividing line between the sections in the rack, and greenhorns like this are made to stow their bags on one side, while other hands are persuaded to use the other end.

There is something going on here that is much more serious than just conning extra rum out of ordinary seamen, and he decides it is time he took a hand. He rises deliberately, and without uttering a word goes across to withdraw his kit-bag from its rack and place it beside that of the newcomer, conscious that all conversation has ceased while the gang stare at him with a mixture of bewilderment and malice.

Malloy moves over to confront Mort. 'If you'll take my advice, mate. You'll put yours back where it belongs.' There is an underlying threat in every word.

'It belongs where I put it,' declares Mort flatly, staring deep into the narrow eyes. 'What difference can it make, anyway?' The question is a challenge.

'It's my responsibility ter keep order 'ere – senior 'ands to the left – others ter the right.'

'Balls!' He spits the word straight into Malloy's face. 'I've been watching you lot, and I know exactly what you're up to. Bastards like you are a menace to the service. How much are you rooking these poor sods to protect them from your thieving mates?' He emphasizes each word, digging at the other man's chest with a horny finger. 'If I lose so much as a lanyard you'll regret it. Just try – that's all.'

Malloy is losing face in front of his cronies, searching his brain for some sort of retaliation that will restore their respect, but in the end he has to resort to bluster. 'Yer can't go abaht accusin' people that way. You've got no soddin' proof; so keep yer nose aht.'

His last words are directed at Mort's back, for the leading hand stalks out of the door to descend the stone stairways and emerge into the bright sunshine. The broad expanse of parade-ground is alive with bustling sailors, and he makes his way to the NAAFI with a sick feeling. The Malloys of this world nauseate him, and he would be in his rights to go to the authorities, but there is no way he can bring himself to shop another killick. He tries to shake the thoughts out of his mind as he broods over his pint of beer. Within a short time he will be away from the barracks and all the lousy intrigues, and suddenly he has a yearning to be at sea again, where there are more important things to occupy a man.

Seven years in the Navy have left few illusions. The war has brought a new element into the service. Most of the HOs are OK and compare well with the regulars once the rough edges are knocked off, but it is inevitable that some rotten apples get into the barrel, and enter the arena as reluctant conscripts, determined to take every opportunity to make life easy for themselves. They sneer at tradition and indulge themselves to the deprivation of others who are less crafty or weaker. They bring with them the wiles and guile of a corrupt past to bribe and blackmail their way into quiet numbers, and for long-service men like Mort, steeped in the customs and unwritten laws that govern the cramped conditions in ships, men like Malloy are as big a menace as the enemy.

'Wotcher, Mort!' He winces as a heavy hand grabs his shoulder to swing him round so that he is looking into the round features of a tubby leading hand. The moon face beams up at him with genuine pleasure at seeing an old shipmate. Wally Singleton stands five feet six in his socks, with a circumference that measures roughly the same. He wobbles like a jelly whenever he laughs, and Wally spends most of his time laughing. Shoulder-high to Mort's six feet, he creases his eyes to stare into the blunt face that looks so forlorn. 'What's up, mate? You've got a face like the arse-end of a camel.'

'You're a sight for sore eyes,' says Mort, breaking into a grin. 'How come you're loafing in barracks?'

'Buy me a pint and I'll tell you.' There is a long pause while he takes his first long, satisfying gulp and sets the glass down. 'My ship paid off a month ago, and I've bin here ever since. I wangled myself a cushy little number in the drafting office – thought I'd never go to sea again, mate. There are barrack-stanchions in that office with three badges on their arms who turn pale at the notion of goin' to sea. The bribery and corruption has to be seen to be believed. Some of the old crowd have bin making a fortune taking pay-offs to keep blokes' records buried.'

'Bloody hell!' exclaims Mort. 'How can you live with a bunch of skates like that?'

'Easy, me old son. My old adage is: "If you can't lick 'em – join 'em." No need to get all aereated though, Mort. Yesterday the sky fell in; a new drafting Master-At-Arms took over, and he's taken the whole system apart – you've never heard such wailing and gnashing of teeth. There'll be some shocks in the next few days, believe me. Here's one bloke that's due for a surprise.' Mort follows the direction of his nod and sees Malloy with some of his mates at the door.

'You know that bastard?'

'Everybody knows him in RNB. He's more famous than Hitler. If there's something really rotten going on, you can bet him and his mates are behind it.' Wally smiles an evil smile.

'But I can tell you he's about to get his come-uppance. He's due for a change of scenery very shortly.'

*

Beside the village that sits like a saddle on top of the Cotswolds, Tom Wordsley straddles the loose stone wall and looks down into the deep valley winding its way towards Wales and the coalfields. His long legs hang loose as he chews straw and watches the silver sheen of the railway tracks running alongside the pea-green water of the old disused canal. This is where he was born, and where he has spent all his life until six months ago, when at the age of seventeen he joined the Navy. Now he lifts his face to the sun as though its warmth can burn away the shock that turns his face grey. In vain he strives to push away the hellish memory that haunts his mind, but it insists on searching out the recesses of his brain to fill it with vivid pictures of the confused agony of the sinking ship and the icy water. The sympathetic crew of the rescue ship had rubbed circulation back into his frozen limbs, and fed life back into his shattered body. It is all a vague kaleidoscope now, the rattling drive through the dockyard and the impersonal routine of barracks, though one small incident stands out clear in his mind: the bearded features of the leading hand who urged them through the clothing centre and ripped a fistful of vest away from his chest. He smiles at the memory. It had been almost an act of violence, yet he could feel the man's compassion.

Far below a long coal-train struggles up the line on its way to the Midlands. Two engines in front, and a banker pushing from behind: they fill the valley with smoke as the sound reaches up to him; solid with power as they climb the gradient. The day is growing old and the first chill breath of evening sends a shiver through him. It is time to move, but he is reluctant to break the spell, for this is the last day of his leave, and he dreads the morrow with its promise of a return to the grey world of steel.

*

Five days' embarkation leave has not improved Malloy's disposition one iota. The draft-chit dropped onto the mess table like a bombshell soon after his confrontation with Mort. In one foul move the Navy destroyed his little empire. He found himself badgered from pillar to post, carrying out his draft routine. It was obvious from the long queues that he was part of a large draft, though there was no mention of his destination. As the day wore on, he had time to ponder over the events leading up to the draft, and the separate incidents began to fit into place like a jig-saw until a picture emerged, showing quite clearly in his twisted mind that there had been a plot against his regime. It started with the set-to with that new killick, the one with the radar badge on his arm, but he was nothing like the poncy sort you would normally expect from that bunch – more like a product from the gunnery school at Whale Island. He had been in deep conversation with that tubby little bloke from the drafting office who took so much delight in handing out the routine form. Put it all together, and in Malloy's mind it has to add up to a conspiracy.

So, on the day when the special train draws up to the platform behind the barracks with its cold, empty carriages, he stands there with his bag-meal, hammock and kit-bag, glaring in the direction of Mort, who is taking charge of a group further down the train. Their kit is stowed into luggage coaches, and all they are allowed to retain are their small, brown attache cases containing a few personal items. Malloy is supposed to regulate his section so that they board the train in some kind of order and locate their seats for the long journey northward. In reality he leaves them to their own devices, using his rank only to ensure that he gets a prime seat, to sit and brood. Where he comes from, it is a point of honour to take reprisals on anyone who upsets a man's prestige, and he will spend the long hours of a boring journey formulating a plan to take revenge.

Mort sorts out his group and takes charge with the minimum of fuss, unaware that one of the youngsters is staring at him with an expression akin to hero-worship. Tom

Wordsley is determined to lick the growing feeling of panic that is gnawing inside his guts, and needs the reassurance of a familiar face, so he ensures that he occupies the seat opposite Mort as he is borne away to a new ship where the messdecks will be filled with nightmarish memories.

At the last moment a flurry of activity draws everyone's eyes to the barrack gate. Confusion is spilling out onto the platform as Wally negotiates the obstacles with a two-wheeled cart piled high with an enormous amount of gear. The little fat man has difficulty keeping the shafts level against the influence of the badly loaded cart. His feet constantly leave the ground as it takes charge, so that he makes progress in a series of uncontrollable swoops, cheered on by a train-load of grinning faces, until the cart comes to rest beside the open door of the baggage car. Sweat pours from his overweight body as he struggles with his kit, and his features take on a crimson hue that would cause alarm in medical circles when he finally manages to stagger free of his load and falls into the arms of Mort, who bundles him into a seat. When he regains his composure he stares about him with distaste until he focuses on Mort's grinning face.

'Would you bloody well credit it!' he exclaims. 'That poxy drafting Master-At-Arms! He confused the system so much I've drafted me fuckin' self!'

*

Dawn finds them eating breakfast in the huge canteen of a Scottish shipyard. During the forenoon they are allocated messes and receive cards with all the details of their duties, watches and actions stations, before being paraded in three ranks on the jetty to stare up at the high flank of their new home. Petty Officer Envoldsen is a gunnery instructor who seems to hate the world. He takes his stance in front of his party of seamen and surveys them with a jaundiced look.

'HMS *Cyclops* is a light fleet carrier – and yer can take that stupid grin orf yer face.' The luckless ordinary seaman who had no idea he was smiling snaps his mouth shut. 'Yer'll ave nuffin' ter laugh at soon, me lad. You're comin' up against a new breed of animal. Somethin' most of yer 'ave never seen before, unless you've served on a carrier. Birdmen! Once we gets ter sea and everyfink is beginning ter look ship-shape and pusser, the aircraft will arrive, along wiv a shower of layabouts the like of which yer can't imagine. They ain't sailors – they ain't airmen. They're a bunch of lousy misfits who don't know a hawser from a yardarm, and before long the whole ship will be a fuckin' shambles. They'll be under yer feet wherever yer goes. We'll do our best ter keep them under control, and away from the parts of ship where the real sailorin' is done, but from time ter time you're bahned ter come inter contact wiv' 'em. It is best ter try and ignore 'em if yer can, and git on wiv yer job; but if any birdman tries ter order yer abaht, yer comes straight ter me or one of yer 'eads of department, and we'll sort 'em aht – no messin'. Nah, get yer kit stowed. Clean inter yer number twos by noon for the commissionin' ceremony on the flight-deck. Till then, I don't want ter see yer skulkin' abaht.' He pulls himself upright to cast a final glare over them before roaring, '*Attention! Turn right! Dismiss!*'

His concern is premature, for a month passes before *Cyclops* is ready to steam out to receive her squadrons. In that time her ship's company have worked day and night to take on stores, fuel and ammunition. Constant drills, exercises and shoots have moulded them into shape, and a growing community spirit is building. She is moored to a buoy off Rothesay when the first lighter of the day brings an advance party of the Fleet Air Arm complement out from shore, and despite efforts by some officers there is a division between the ship's company and the squadron personnel.

Many of the regular senior hands with backgrounds in battle-ships, cruisers and the like do little to improve the situation, for they do not take kindly to service in a 'floating aerodrome'. A month is time enough for the crew to become a family; and to have an influx of newcomers suddenly thrust amongst them, with a vocabulary and a way of life alien to their own, is hard to accept. A far-sighted command would have seen the problems that will arise if the situation is allowed to continue, but nothing is done to heal the division, with the result that as time goes by the two factions will become even more set in their individual ways, and for once marines, stokers and seamen forget their traditional differences and become allied against the airmen.

The morning after the newcomers arrive the ship is under sailing orders, and 'Special Sea Dutymen' is broadcast over the tannoy as a grey dawn spreads reluctantly from the bleak hills to the east. Malloy is coxswain of the second motor cutter, and clambers down over the starboard boom with his crew and a couple of buoy-jumpers. He is hung-over and morose, snarling orders as they slip the painter to approach the buoy. A brisk wind comes in from the open sea to make things difficult for the two men who have to leap across to the slippery surface of the buoy and unshackle the heavy 'bridle', so that it can be heaved back inboard and re-secured to the starboard anchor.

Malloy is in no mood for refinements, and drives the bow of his cutter straight at the buoy, winding the wheel of the Kitchener gear to put her astern at the last possible moment. The boat strikes the buoy a heavy, glancing blow, so that the two seamen have to hang on for dear life to keep from being flung into the water and crushed by the cutter. The opportunity is lost, and Malloy slates them for their puny efforts before taking the boat out in a wide sweep to make a second approach.

Looking down from the fo'c'sle, Mort, Envoldsen and the lieutenant in charge make no comment about his inept antics. Another coxswain would have made his approach slowly up-wind to make things easy as possible for the two men. Not Malloy. His method is to swing in with as much speed as possible to make the cutter more responsive to the helm, but the bucket-gear has to be closed round the propeller at the critical moment to reverse the thrust and stop her in time. Once in every ten times a coxswain will get away with this mindless method, but today everything was goes wrong. The gap is still wide when the first man suddenly goes astern. In order to try to save himself he attempts to leap the gap, only to fall into the sea where he has to struggle desperately to stay clear of the plunging bow.

Ten minutes is wasted while Malloy makes clumsy efforts to recover the man and put him back on board again before he begins to suffer from exposure. Meanwhile angry phone-calls from the bridge demand to know the reason for the hold-up. After an angry exchange with the lieutenant, PO Envoldsen orders Mort to take Malloy's place in the boat. There are few things more humiliating than a boat's coxswain being relieved for incompetence, especially when it takes place under the critical eyes of most of his colleagues. So when the two men change places in the sternsheets Malloy is shaking with suppressed rage, and his hand stays clamped on the tiller for a long time while he fights to control himself. Mort is in no mood for histrionics, and wrenches it away with his set features inches from the other man's venomous eyes. It takes a sharp command from an officer at the top of the ladder to break the confrontation and force sanity into Malloy.

Fifteen minutes later *Cyclops* is ready to slip. The marine bugler sounds a single 'G' over the tannoy and the blacksmith's maul crashes down onto the blake-slip to release the single wire holding the carrier to the buoy. The Jack flutters down from its staff, and pennant numbers stream up to the yardarm. In one brief moment she is transformed from a ship at her mooring to a ship at sea, with her screws churning a maelstrom as they push her twenty-four thousand tons in a wide sweep to point her bow towards the open sea.

The bugle sounds again, this time bringing the crew to 'action stations', and Mort makes his way up to the small cabin at the base of the 'island'. Inside is housed the 79b radar set. It is treated by most of his fellow operators as something of a joke, for alongside the up-to-date sophisticated equipment in the Air Direction Room and on the bridge, it is archaic. There are no PPIs here with their all-round scanners that rotate with the aerials mounted high on the masts to paint full displays of the surrounding areas. In front of Mort as he sits in his swivel-chair is a control that is an exact replica of the steering-wheel of a London bus. When he turns it a parabolic reflector rotates to probe the atmosphere with a finger of pulsating energy until it is bounced back from a piece of solid matter. He stares into an 'A' scan with a thin green line glowing across the centre of its three-inch dial, and when a contact is made an alpine peak grows out of the 'grass'. In order to find the bearing of this 'echo', he must rotate his aerial from the point where the peak is barely visible until it almost disappears again, before swinging back to the half-way point – that should be the approximate bearing of his target. It compares to its modern counterpart like the Camel of the First World War compares with the Spitfire, and a man needs great faith to take it seriously. Mort has faith; in fact, it has become his baby. One day he knows the single-minded concentration of its tunnel-vision will surprise them all.

Today he is visited by Lieutenant Luxley-Hamilton, who swims inside an ill-fitting uniform that drapes loosely over his bony frame, making him look like a moth-eaten vulture. He peers over Mort's shoulder at the set with a devoted expression, for, like Mort, he has a special affection for this set. He can almost feel the energy pulses leaping out from its heart as the leading hand searches the horizon. He leans across to make a fine adjustment to the tuning before standing back satisfied. Mort concentrates hard, hoping he will go away, for one of the perks of this job is that a man is left alone, and he resents being watched over like an OD.

The lieutenant comes from a very privileged background, but prides himself on treating everyone as his equal. Back home where his father owns most of the village nestling just below his huge estate he has earned himself a reputation for being a meddlesome busybody amongst the disgruntled inhabitants, for he insists on joining them in the fields and the pub at every opportunity. His one aim in life is to be loved by all.

'Have you had any experience with Gazebos, Mortimer?' he asks. 'We are having terrible trouble with the one at home. Rusting all over the place.'

Mort grabs the opportunity with both hands. 'Not really, sir. My old man's got a small Morris eight, but he doesn't seem to get any real trouble with it.'

The officer is used to being misinterpreted, and the earphones clamped on Mort's head must make hearing difficult, but it has the desired effect, and the leading hand is grateful to find himself left in solitude once more. He feels the deck vibrate as revolutions build up and the carrier leans almost imperceptibly as she swings into the wind. He can hear the wind building up as her speed increases, and the two crash-barriers thump into position just outside his office. Several peaks lift out of the 'grass' and he reports the new contacts with their ranges and bearings, only to be told that they are already plotted on the big, perspex screen in the ADR. Sod them all! One day he'll floor the bloody lot of them!

*

To Lieutenant-Commander Potter *Cyclops* looks surprisingly large after the pocket-sized escort carriers he is used to. The affirmative flag is hoisted to show she is ready to receive her aircraft, and he leads his group of four Corsairs up the starboard side, flying abreast at mast height. Close enough to see faces staring at them from the 'island'. No theatricals today. Everything must be done by the book, or he will need to know the reason why. A green light comes from the carrier and he banks over to run down her port side. The sleek destroyer doing duty as 'crash-boat' maintains her station off the starboard quarter, with her sea-boat swung out and the oars manned, ready to pick up any luckless airman who has to ditch. 'Not today,' he promises himself, wriggling his backside more comfortably on the one-man dinghy sandwiched between his buttocks and his parachute. He banks again to line up for his final approach. Already his number two is following down the port side, and the second flight of four is roaring up the starboard flank as though they are on review. He concentrates on 'Bats' as the carrier looms ahead, and gets the 'cut' before thumping down easily on to her deck.

The crash-barriers slump down as men come at him from all sides. He is waved on by a marshal, and the engine roars as he opens the throttle to taxi forward to the parking area, where Leading Aircraftman Tibbet waits to help him out of the cockpit. He hurries towards the 'island', for the golden rule is to get off the flight-deck as quickly as possible when landing on. Just inside the entrance he is met by the Air Staff Officer.

'Come up to the bridge, Bertie, and meet some of the salt-horses. A good show today might do a lot for public relations.'

'Is there room for improvement then?'

ASO gives a wry grin. 'You could say that. There are some hard-nosed traditionalists on board who believe the ultimate weapon is the fifteen-inch gun.'

On the bridge the atmosphere is coldly polite as they watch the aircraft making their final approaches. It all goes well until the last Corsair comes winging down the port side. The hook and under-carriage are lowered and locked as he comes abreast, and it looks as though he is going to round off the day with a perfect landing.

Potter watches apprehensively, for he has a sudden premonition. This pilot is a flamboyant character with more skill than brain, and something tells the squadron leader that he is about to make an entrance. Not for him the orthodox approach. During the time they have spent with the escort carrier they have perfected a modified version by using a split circuit. It was developed to perfection, and everyone knew exactly what to do. Today *Cyclops* is about to be treated to her premier performance, and she is totally unprepared for it.

Dropping his port wing the pilot brings his Corsair round in a tight turn, then seems to hover suspended over the stern before side-slipping on to the flight-deck. It would have been successful too, had not *Cyclops* decided to drop her stern ten feet at the most critical moment. 'Bats' desperately tries to wave him off, but he is committed. The engine cuts as he crosses the arresting wires, and the aircraft drops like a stone to hit the deck and bounce clean over the wires and the barriers, splaying the undercarriage before sliding out of control into the mass of parked aircraft. When the noise and chaos subsides it is the only one left on the flight-deck, and a trail of upturned tail-planes and broken fuselages stretches out astern in the turbulence of the carrier's wake.

The destroyer's seaboat is lowered in record time and pulled in amongst the flotsam in search of the one casualty, but Leading Aircraftman Tibbet has been trodden underfoot by the giant ship, and churned to mincemeat by her propellers. Eight aircraft have been written off in one go by an act of irresponsibility, and it does nothing to improve the image of the Fleet Air Arm. The escort returns to her station, and *Cyclops* turns for home. The ship's company goes to 'defence stations' as the bugler sounds 'cooks to the galley'.

*

Three messes run side by side on the seamen's messdeck, with rows of lockers lining the bulkheads. Mort is in charge of the centre one while Malloy and Wally watch over his neighbours. The passage that runs forward past the inboard ends of the tables is a busy thoroughfare leading to the forward messdecks. A procession of cooks troop by, carrying trays of food from the galley. The talk is of the events on the flight-deck, and embarrassed airmen have to run the gauntlet of derisive comments as they hurry forward with their rations.

Cyclops seems determined to widen the rift as she pulls one of her bloody-minded stunts, choosing the moment when a luckless airman is passing with a container of thick stew to roll heavily and send him sprawling across the end of Malloy's table. The glutinous mess splatters over everything and everyone to a chorus of indignant shouts, and he finishes up standing sheepishly amid the debris, mouthing fervent apologies.

'Fuckin' birdmen!' raves Malloy, bulldozing his way through the mess to wrench the empty fanny from the airman's hands and ram it into his chest beneath his nose. 'Sod orf and get some more 'ot water in this, yer little wart, then come back ere and scrub away yer filth!'

'Sorry, Hooky,' blurts the delinquent. 'Can I get another lot for me own mess first?'

'Can yer 'ell, yer cheeky little bastard! If yer not back in three minutes I'll wrap that fanny rahnd yer scrawny neck!'

Unable to stay quiet any longer, Tom Wordsley takes the container from the lad. 'It's okay, mate. It wasn't your fault: I'll clean this lot up.' He turns to go aft.

Everyone is watching now, and Malloy, fully aware that he holds centre stage, intends to show them all that he won't be messed about. He wrests the fanny back and slams it into the airman's midriff. 'I'm tellin' yer ter get the water – *now!*' He turns to Wordsley. 'And as fer you. Keep yer snotty nose aht!'

There is an awkward silence and Mort sits watching across a plate of stew. What takes places in another man's mess is none of his affair, but the situation is turning sour now and affecting everyone.

The airman returns in record time with his steaming water and Wordsley automatically begins to clear away utensils with another member of the mess to allow the lad to wash down the end of the table. Malloy leaps up, his features suffused with rage. 'I told yer ter leave it alone!' he roars, and swipes the OD with a back-hander that sends him sprawling back into his mates.

Mort scrambles over the table to place himself between the two of them. 'You're sailing close to the wind, Malloy.'

'Keep yer nose aht!'

'Simmer down, for Christ's sake. You can get done for hitting a junior rating.'

Malloy is breathing heavily, but some reason returns as he looks from one to the other before shrugging, 'I'm not that stupid. This little sod will clean up his filth though: I'll see ter that!'

'It was an accident. Shave off, mate, you've had your money's worth. Let him get back to his mess.'

It hangs in the air for a few seconds. Everyone focusing on Malloy's twitching features. The scene is frozen when a leading aircraftman arrives to find one of his men scrubbing the deck.

'What goes on here?' he demands, tightlipped. 'I spilt some grub when I fell,' explains the youngster, anxious not to build the thing up again. 'I'm just clearing it up before I get some more.'

'You're taking your time about it. I don't like to see one of my lads cleaning up for a bunch of bloody dabtoes.'

Mort stops Malloy just in time, warning the leading airman, 'You'd better shove off, mate, before you start something you can't finish.' He grabs the fanny from the lad. 'Here, we'll attend to this. Go back where you belong.'

When they have gone Malloy turns on Mort. 'That's the second time yer've made an idiot aht of me. There won't be a third.'

'No one needs to make an idiot out of you, Malloy. You make a good job of that yourself – you'll wind up in chokey one day if you carry on the way you are.'

They are still facing up to each other when Petty Officer Envoldsen comes in with his cap in his hand. 'Don't like disturbin' you in your mess, lads, but I've changed some duties. As from today Mortimer will coxswain the second motor cutter at harbour stations, and you'll be on the fo'c'sle with me, Malloy.' Without further ado he spins on his heel and strides out, leaving behind an atmosphere that could be cut with a knife.

TWO

Abbé Le Clerq pushes the heavy, studded door shut, relishing the feel of the ancient timber, for it is said that this is all that remains of the original church that stood here when Normandy was in its heyday, and religion had its rightful place in the way of things. Once the old church stood in the centre of the village, until the plague came and ravaged the countryside. In fear the population had burned down their houses along with the corpses before building a new village two kilometres away. The surrounding ground still shows undulations and mounds to mark the spot where the houses once stood. Now a scourge of another kind dominates the countryside, wearing the grey uniforms of an occupying army.

At first when the Germans came, the church was filled with worshippers each Sunday, and prayers for a liberated France rocked the old eaves. Brave words proclaimed the determination of the locals to resist the Boche until freedom was restored. Since then the congregation has dwindled, along with the fine words and the will to fight. True, there are factions who carry out surreptitious raids and acts of sabotage, but they are mainly political groups and malcontents with axes to grind, using the system to gain their own ends. They are condemned by villager and German alike for rocking the boat and making things even more arduous when restrictions are imposed so that people cannot go about their business in peace. Those who run the affairs of the community would be outraged if anyone accused them of collaboration: passive resistance is the term for their acquiescence. They fool nobody, least of all themselves.

There is a change in the air though. A new feeling that seems to waft in on the sea wind as it batters the lofty cliffs to send fingers of spray lifting up the crevices like the clutching hands of a besieging army, and it brings with it an excitement that sets the adrenalin flowing. Rumours abound, and the relationship between occupier and occupied is more restrained. Curfew is stringently maintained. Two days ago the curé had watched a convoy of cars and trucks grind inland from the coast road to halt five hundred metres from the church. Hidden from view in the porch he saw a square man in a long leather coat, high-peaked cap, and the red-striped trousers of a general pointing a baton in various directions, while another made notes. At one time the baton pointed straight at the church and a cold hand seemed to clutch at the curé's heart.

Now as he turns from his door his ears catch the note of an engine struggling in low gear as it climbs the steep hill leading up from the village, and sending that same cold feeling coursing through his insides. He wears his black hair close-cropped over a serious, sallow face. There are sagging pouches beneath his brown eyes, and lines deeply etched that run from wide nostrils to a loose, thick-lipped mouth. In his dark, clerical garb he is a sombre figure, but beneath it all he has a strong rebellious spirit that manifests in outbursts of anger at times when he is frustrated by the double standards set by those who should lead the simple peasants through the years of turmoil. Gradually he has been ostracised because he is an embarrassment to them. The truth he tells them is that they are like lost sheep, sitting so hard on the fence it is a wonder they do not split up the middle.

The vehicle comes into view through the tall poplars lining the road, and casting stark shadows across its dusty surface, so that the big staff-car drives through a corrugation of light and dark until it sweeps into the square in front of the church round the cenotaph, and crunches to a halt under the steady gaze of Saint Christophe, standing in his shrine near the gate. The tall figure of Hauptmann Becq leads the way, followed by

Conseiller Dupont, who considers himself patriarch of the village, where he sways his grey head sagely over local politics. Etienne Martin scurries at his heels like the obedient little puppy that he is. He runs the bicycle-shop when he is not running errands for the illustrious conseiller. Two metres behind, and keeping their distance, two more German officers bring up the rear. They are strangers to the priest, but he can recognise the uniforms of the SS. They look about them as though they expect gunmen to jump out from behind the old tombstones, and take no part in the exchange of greetings.

Dupont comes straight to the point once the niceties are done. 'There is a new directive, Monsieur le curé. Not only is the coast out of bounds to us, but it has become necessary to evacuate all outlying farms and buildings on the headland from noon today. It is for the safety of the civilian population as much as for military purposes you understand. You will have to come and live in the village with us.'

The priest looks at the bland faces. All these people just to tell him that? It makes no sense. Etienne is shuffling about nervously, unable to meet his eyes, and there is a shadow of guilt in the conseiller's face. 'There is more to it than that, Henri.'

Dupont drops his gaze for a second before staring straight into the priest's face. 'The church will have to close too.'

Le Clerq's features harden. 'The church has not closed for centuries. It is the heart of the community.'

'It also stands on the highest point of the headland,' explains Becq, not unkindly. 'It is a military matter, priest.'

'What are you going to do to my church?' the curé demands suspiciously.

The Hauptmann is becoming impatient. 'That is not your concern, priest.' He relents a little. 'War is unkind to us all, Father. At home churches, schools, hospitals have been bombed by the RAF. A small country church is of no real consequence.'

Realisation dawns. 'You are going to destroy it.'

In the background Major Kurt Müller has had enough. He

speaks very little French, and has no time for the Wehrmacht, especially those like Becq who are living out the war amongst French peasants while he and his kind are doing all the fighting. He is young for a major, with a dark, handsome face that is loth to smile, and there is a look in his eyes that betrays a cruel streak. He is a product of Hitler's Third Reich. The son of a builders' merchant, who would never have risen above the rank of sergeant in the Wehrmacht. He is part of an advance party of the 21st SS Armoured Divison, and his Panthers have driven north from Brittany, leaving a trail of broken tarmac. They have been 'cleaning up' villages all the way, over-riding the milk-sop methods of the occupying forces. He fumes as the talk goes on.

'We have no time for this nonsense, Hauptmann. Tell the fool to pack a bag and come with us.'

The curé may not understand the language, but the meaning is quite clear. They are taken unawares when he makes a sudden dash for the door, heaving it shut behind him, and shooting the heavy bolts. The church was built as much for sanctuary as for worship in a time when there were others who would destroy it. So it is like a fortress, even to the battlements on the tower.

'Destroy the church, and you will have to destroy me!' he shouts at them from within the porch.

'Don't be a fool,' warns Dupont. 'We will build you a new church when the war is over.'

All they hear is muffled sounds echoing from inside, but no more words. The Hauptmann slaps his side angrily. 'I will get a party of troopers up from the village to weed him out.'

'No, you won't. The SS will take care of it.' The major's tone allows no argument as he turns to his second-in-command, leading him down the path towards the staff-car, talking earnestly all the way. The Leutnant nods and barks an order to the driver, who takes a field telephone from the back seat of the car and mouths instructions. Müller turns away from them all, deliberately ignoring them as he stands with his hands clasped behind his back, contemplating the ancient church with calculating eyes.

Inside the tower Le Clerq flattens hard against the wall

listening. The voices are muffled and confused and he cannot understand a word. Above him the wind moans mournfully through the belfry and seems to reach down into his soul. He has no idea what to do next, just an empty feeling inside. He has seen France shamed and humiliated throughout the past four years and can endure it no longer. There has been a place of worship here for over a thousand years and that evil uniformed heathen is not going to find it easy to demolish it. He backs slowly up the stone stairway. His isolation closes in on him up here where the wind blusters through the roof and the big bell hangs mute, draped with cobwebs while thick dust gathers everywhere. The narrow slit of an embrasure frames an elongated view of the valley, stretching out beyond the tops of the trees to where the river threads through a patchwork of meadows with cattle grazing contentedly at the rich grass. The raucous chatter of rooks supersedes all else until he stiffens at a new sound growing from the direction of the village. The clink of metal tracks, and the heavy roar of big diesels sends a chill through him.

His mind should turn to prayer, but there is no room for that here, for his motives are not priestly and he must face this ordeal alone. God has no part in these affairs, where men stand by and look on while a nation tears out the soul of a continent at the whim of a maniac. Le Clerq is not acting the part of a priest now, and the black thoughts that dominate his mind are far from religious. He is consumed with an overpowering hate, a lust to take revenge on these persecutors.

He pulls himself into the narrow aperture to look down towards the road where two massive tanks are wallowing through the dust towards the church. They rumble into the square, and he watches as they grind the cenotaph into the dirt and come to rest with engines idling, purring like two contented cats waiting for the mice to come out to play. Filled with dread he backs away from the embrasure to cower in a corner of the timber floor beneath the heavy preponderance of the bell. The engines stop, and an all-consuming silence pervades the atmosphere for a moment before he hears the whine of electric motors as they train their guns round. The curé's heart pounds while he holds his breath and bows his head into folded arms.

'You have ten seconds, priest!'

He sucks in his breath. Now he starts to pray. Selfish prayers, pleading for strength – mercy – forgiveness – anything to relieve him from the terror that drains his insides. He has only to shout or wave a hand from the embrasure to end the torture, but his muscles are frozen as he buries his head deeper into the black folds of his habit. *'Notre Père'*, he begins to recite quickly, the words tumbling from his trembling lips in an incoherent cascade. He gasps as the blast of the first gun reverberates through the church.

Methodically they blast the granite walls, starting at the east end, demolishing the altar and working towards the tower where Müller knows instinctively the priest is hiding. Before the shells reach the base of the tower he orders: 'Cease fire!' and allows the dust and rubble to subside before calling out, 'There is no church now, priest. Come out while you still can.' Becq's throat is dry as he translates.

Le Clerq lifts his head. The stench of explosives stings his nostrils, and dust clogs his mouth. A cold rage takes hold of him. A blind hate for a world gone mad, and for a religion that is impotent when its servant cries for help. He pushes back against the wall and straightens his legs to force his body upright before reaching for the rope. He swings his full weight onto it, and slowly the bell begins to sway. The clapper finds the rim with a deep sound that reaches across the valley. People stop and look towards the church. Troops grip their weapons more tightly and look to authority for guidance. The bell rings out over the fields, yet the skies are clear and there is no sign of an invasion that should follow such a warning.

Müller grins at his second-in-command and nods. The engines burst into life and the first tank rumbles towards the tower. It smashes into the granite, cracking the brittle stone and tearing a gash in the wall. Its partner positions itself for a final thrust that must surely bring down the tower. The bell

stops ringing and the Hauptmann yells angrily at Müller to
hold the second Panther, then goes over to the gap to shout up
into the dust:

'It is over now, priest. Come down while you can.'

He kicks loose stone from the stairway and begins to climb
warily until he can see the timbered roof and the dying swing
of the big bell. Clouds of dust hang heavy in the bleak light,
and Le Clerq stoops with the rope slack in his hands, a figure
of utter dejection. Part of the lower wall suddenly crumples to
remind the Hauptmann of their danger. 'Come,' he urges.
'You can do no more. You will have us both killed.'

The priest allows himself to be led down the steps into the
sunshine. Müller fidgets impatiently, waiting until they are
clear before he waves the second tank in. It seems to carve
through the stone as though it is chalk, ripping out another
corner as it trundles out to crush old gravestones beneath its
giant tracks. The tower totters undecided for a second before
slowly toppling over, holding its shape until it hits the ground
to spread its length across the graveyard. The curé is led to the
staff-car by the Hauptmann, where he sits in silence as they
drive down into the village. The houses are square and without
character, clustered together as though they would like to hide
from the sun, and one has to look into corners to find the
villagers these days for they tend to remain in the shadows. A
faded Byhrr advert decorates the gable of a barn to mark the
beginning of the village, and a low bridge over the Orne marks
the end. It is a rock-strewn trickle of a stream, barely enough
to wash away the garbage that is thrown into it. Peacetime
travellers hurry through towards Caen, hoping for better
things, and only the man at the petrol pumps ever gets to meet
a stranger. Most of the inhabitants prefer it that way, content
to go about their affairs without interference or advice from
those who sneer at their lethargy and peasant ways. They are
happy to allow the seasons and the soil to dictate the pace of
life, and it is small wonder that they are apathetic while the
turmoil of war goes on about them. Even when news of the
destruction of their church reaches them they pass it off with a

few outraged comments and lukewarm anger, for today they draw their ration of tobacco and that only happens every tenth day.

Much to his annoyance Etienne is to play host to the curé until proper accommodation can be found. Dupont waves aside his objections, and Le Clerq is too numb to protest. Müller's Panthers are driven into the trees verging the roadway, and the crews are busy camouflaging them with branches and netting. Tomorrow they will be deployed about the countryside. Hidden in barns, outbuildings and haystacks. Even the grass will be mown to erase their tracks, and from the air it will look as though they never existed. The small barracks just clear of the village has SS sentries on the gate, and most of the patrols are Müller's men. A new order has taken over, and people hurry about their chores, eager to be back in the sanctuary of their homes. The local garrison withdraw into themselves, reluctant to be seen fraternising, and there is tension in the air.

*

Long after curfew Nicole Martin lies awake in her bed, staring at the blue shadows on the ceiling. She stretches her long legs full length so that her toes peek out from the bedclothes. When she runs her hands down over her body she can feel the firmness of her stomach and the taut muscles of her thighs. At nineteen her breasts are well developed, but her buttocks are not as full and rounded as she would like. Sometimes her father laughs when she bends her arm to show strong biceps: for she revels in sport and physical exercise, and it sets her apart from the dumpy village girls. Her mind too is active, and now it wrestles with her jumbled thoughts as she lies there with the moonlight streaming in through the small window. She should have grown used to her father's indolence by now, but it rankles when he neglects his shop. The customers are used to searching him out at the local wine bar, for her mother's dominating influence sends him scurrying off at every opportunity to join his little clique.

What galls her most, however, is the way he toadies to Dupont and his circle of fellow collaborators, who have feathered their nests in the new regime, even to the extent of denouncing undesirables to the Germans. When she raises her voice in protest both her parents become outraged and accuse her of being too young to understand. At such times she sees real anxiety in her father's eyes, and she knows that inside he is like a jelly. She despises him for his weakness, yet she pities him also, for he is a very simple man.

She stirs restlessly. She hates the Germans, and even more those who pander to them. They cannot know the real reason for her contempt of the enemy and the pretentious men in the village who talked loud, but did nothing. She was just sixteen and the occupation had only just begun when she heard the sound that drew her to the window where she could see down into the back-yard of the house next door. The moon had been full and bright that night, bright enough to see into the shadows and the German soldier with his breeches slumped down over his jackboots. His pale backside gleamed in the moon's glow as he thrust hard between the ample thighs of Camille. Now she blushes furiously as she recalls how she could not wait to whisper the tale to her friends, and the way they listened eagerly to every morsel in a giggling group. She couldn't speak to Camille afterwards without a certain awe, and she lay for long periods 'twixt waking and sleeping, filled with visions that stirred emotions that had hitherto lain dormant.

Now she is older, and the memory remains clear in her mind, but the excitement is dead. She has tasted 'love' as they call it. Clumsy, hurtful, even bestial, with Marcel who drives the coal lorry into Caen every week. In a strange way Camille had a hand in that too, for it took place only months after the episode in the back-yard while the vision was still fresh. Curiosity led her into allowing him to fondle her, and when it came to stopping him she had let things go too far. He was like a mad bull; and afterward, when he lay back and realised that he was the first, he had no remorse, but grinned at her and gloated. Soon every male in the village knew about it, for he went about bragging of his conquest. She found herself pestered by other louts who thought she would be easy and were affronted when they found themselves rebuffed. She earned herself a reputation for being a shrew.

She had contempt for all men. The weak ones like her father, the uncouth ones like Marcel, but most of all the arrogant soldiers of the Third Reich. She was filled with loathing to the extent that she found it impossible to hide her feelings when she met them in the street. Sometimes she was so outspoken her parents pleaded with her to think of them and contain herself, but she found there were others just like her who felt as strongly as she did about the invaders, and it was not long before she became involved with members of resistance groups. At first she did no more than circulate copies of *Combat*, smuggled out of Paris by railwaymen, but since the beginning of 1944 the Allies have been dropping increased quantities of arms and supplies and the rebels have become more brazen. She has proved herself braver than most men, and willing to undertake almost any task; indeed, she angers many when she threatens their secret operations with her recklessness. The Allied Command will not support irresponsible guerrilla activity to undermine the overall strategy. Hotheads like Nicole alert the Germans and are a threat to the resistance, so she has been pushed further and further into the background.

The Germans are alive to the growing threat of the Maquisard and rumours circulate every day telling of reprisals and draconian measures being used to crush uprisings and sabotage. The SS take hostages at random and set up firing parties where they suspect underground activity, and the arrival of Müller's Panthers sends a thrill of fear through the village. The major makes no bones about the prime purpose for his presence, or the utter contempt he has for the soft approach of the local garrison. His men patrol the roads, stopping people and searching them indiscriminately, but up to now the only sign of resistance has been the puny effort of the priest that is treated more like an act of an eccentric than a partisan. The major would almost welcome some kind of retaliation for the way he desecrated the church, but apart from a lot of whisperings and dark looks their reaction has been gutless. His Panthers are wasted here in this backwater. Everyone knows the real fighting will take place a lot further north where the channel is narrow, and less unpredictable, and the enemy can rely on close air support. While Nicole fidgets in her bed he sits with his maps and considers where best to laager his tanks.

The first priority is the setting up of the radar station. It is the responsibility of the Kriegsmarine, and they say they can complete the installation in two to three weeks if the site is clear. Müller has done what the Wehrmacht seemed reluctant to do and demolished most of the church. Soon the big Würzburg Riese will raise its 7.4 metre parabolic reflector over the landscape to search out a radius of up to 65,000 metres. The SS major has little time for the technicalities of it all, but he can appreciate the importance of this electronic eye in the vast complex of the Atlantic wall.

The days pass without incident, and the village goes on sleeping, even when the troops are put on full alert from time to time when alarms, real or imagined, are raised. Le Clerq moves into a small cottage close to one of the outlying farms, and no one sees anything of him until the following Sunday when a man approaches along the north road wearing a light grey suit with open-necked shirt and beret. A stranger is always an event, so interest mounts as he comes across the bridge, and eyes widen when they recognise the curé, and soon the whole place is alive with watchers gaping unashamedly at the small figure who seems oblivious to them all as he steers a course for Etienne's house. Nicole stands on the threshold filled with curiosity while Etienne peers nervously over her shoulder.

Becq has his quarters in what was once a baker's shop. The walls are lined with detailed maps of the surrounding area, and various charts relating to the disposition of his forces. The previous occupant went off with his unit at the outset of the war and no one knows where he is, or even if he still lives. Now Müller and the Hauptmann face each other across a heavy mahogany desk in an attempt to deploy their troops to mutual advantage. It is a strained discussion, and Becq has great difficulty restraining his anger at the arrogant demands and implications levelled at him, even though he has to admit to himself that relations between his soldiers and the community have been influenced by years of fraternising with the simple, easy-going villagers. Nevertheless he resents any suggestion of lassitude when it comes to carrying out their duties, and stresses that the relationship could be construed as a definite advantage, for he has not had any serious guerilla activity in his area. They exchange looks when the noise and bustle suddenly subsides. Becq goes to the window to peer out onto a strange scene where everyone seems to be staring towards the north. Even the patrols are standing with their eyes fixed towards the bridge, and the centre of attention appears to be a nondescript, shabbily-dressed man shuffling along through the pools of sunlight filtering into the street from the gaps between the houses, heading towards the Martins' home.

'It is the priest,' he says in a puzzled tone, 'and he is not wearing his habit.'

Müller joins him. 'What is he up to?'

Becq shrugs. 'No church – no duty, I suppose. Strange, though. I would expect a priest to stay a priest.' He scans the whole length of the street. The expressionless features of the inhabitants tell him nothing. 'I do not like it; he could become a nuisance.'

'Do something about it then.' The major's face is taunting. 'Or is it to be left to the SS again?'

'Do what, Herr Major? He is walking along the street. What crime is there in that? Anyway,' he adds with a casual wave of his hand, 'he is going to the Martin house. Etienne Martin is afraid of his own shadow. There is no point in stirring things up without cause.'

'Pah!' explodes Müller in exasperation. 'You cannot trust any of the bastards. Do they have to jump out at you with a gun before you react? We are being stabbed in the back wherever we go in this cursed country, Becq. You cannot afford to wait.'

The curé pushes his way through Etienne's door without comment. After the bright sunlight the room is gloomy and obscure. It takes time for his eyes to adjust until the profusion of cheap ornaments that adorn the walls comes into focus. Madame Martin stares belligerently at him from the cavernous fireplace where something simmers pungently, while Etienne and Nicole stand behind him with their backs to the closed door.

'What are you dressed like that for?' asks Etienne bluntly, his nerves showing in his fidgeting hands and worried eyes. 'The whole village is watching. Why do you come here?'

'Be silent!' snarls his wife. 'That is no way to talk to the curé. Make yourself useful and pour some wine.'

'I wish to speak with you, Nicole. I won't intrude any longer than I need to, but I must talk to you alone.'

'Nonsense!' snarls the woman. 'There are no secrets in this house, *mon père*. If you have something to say, you can say it in front of us all.' She glares at Etienne when he seems about to interrupt and he succumbs obediently.

Nicole stays in the shadows, watching Le Clerq curiously. He spreads his hands hopelessly on the table, staring at the hearth. 'In that case, I will have to find some other way. The fewer people who become involved the better.'

'What are you saying?' bursts out Etienne anxiously. 'What can you possibly have to say to Nicole that cannot be heard by us all?' He looks from one to the other, trying to read whatever it is that passes between them.'

No one is more bewildered than Nicole. She has had little to do with the priest, and even when he spent the few hours in their house she kept well out of the way as she does with all of her father's cronies. She leaves the shadows to sit opposite him. 'What can you want with me? I do not even come to your church.'

He glances quickly at her then looks away again. 'It has nothing to do with the church. You may or may not be able to help me, but I cannot speak in front of your family, and I have no one else to turn to.'

'Forget it then!' snaps the dragon viciously.

'No,' says Nicole quietly, as though her mother's outburst is all the incentive she needs. 'I will walk with you to the bridge: we can talk on the way.'

Ignoring their protests she leads him out into the sunshine and they walk together side by side past curious villagers and suspicious soldiers. He seems weighed down with his problem and they reach the bridge before he finds his words. 'Camille Renouf came to see me. She is in trouble, and seems to think you have contacts that could help me to solve her problem.'

Her stomach tightens and she is unable to prevent a momentary surge of fear showing on her face. If he notices he makes no comment, just walking on with his head down, waiting for her to absorb his words and reply. 'I don't know what she is talking about.'

'I know it is difficult – even dangerous, but if you know anyone.' He leaves it hanging in the air, going on ahead while she follows undecided. The village is left behind now. The grass verges are grey with dry dust, while the road in front shimmers in the heat.

'Camille is a slut!' she exclaims harshly. 'She goes with the Germans. I am not surprised she comes to you; she knows full well what to expect when liberation comes.'

'One German,' he corrects evenly. 'She goes with one German.'

'That is more than enough. She is like a lot of others now that they can see which way the wind is blowing. They need to take stock of themselves.'

'I am concerned only for her. She says she wishes to be married when it is all over, and the man is from Alsace – he is not a real German.'

'Is that what she tells you? He wears a German uniform: he is one of them all right.' She laughs bitterly.

He waits while she catches up with him before looking at her. His face is deadly serious, staring into her eyes as though he is trying to read her soul. 'I know it is so, Nicole. She is pregnant, and he is hiding in my house.'

'A deserter!' she exclaims wide-eyed. 'You must be mad! It is the death penalty for anyone who shelters a deserter.'

'That's right, Nicole.' He watches her face intently. 'Now it is up to you. If you do not denounce me you will be party to it all and face the same penalty. You know what they are like. If Camille doesn't involve you, I will probably do so under pressure. There is nothing very heroic about me, I'm afraid.'

'Yet you do not mind implicating others. You should not have listened to her.'

The sound of an engine grows from the direction of the village, and it serves to spur them on again. They reach the lane that leads away from the main road towards the cottage, expecting the vehicle to roar past on its way towards Caen as they turn into it. The sound increases until it nears the junction, then the gears change and they know it is turning into the lane behind them. They stare stolidly ahead, neither wishing to look back as they wait for it to pass. The small Citroen stops a few metres further on, and a sergeant climbs out to come towards them, while two others soldiers watch the countryside with sub-machine guns loose in their hands.

'Major Müller wishes to speak with you, priest. You are to come with us.' He leers at Nicole as Le Clerq obeys. 'I would not stray too far from the village if I were you,' he grins, speaking perfect French. 'Who knows what might happen to you.'

The car reverses into a gateway, then turns back for the village. Only the sergeant looks at her as they drive past. The others sit bolt upright with Le Clerq sitting between them. She is still staring after them when the sound of the engine dies to leave an empty silence, before the birds take up their song. Nicole takes a step or two towards the main road, hesitates, then turns and directs her footsteps towards the cottage.

*

Le Clerq is filled with trepidation as they drive towards the village. These men are Müller's, and their impassive faces make him uncomfortable. He misses the sense of protection his priest's habit gives. These robots of the Führer have a respect for uniforms, and to them his religious attire is no more than that. However superficial its protection might be, he feels naked and vulnerable in this shabby suit. The houses close in about them with blinkered windows and hostile doors, and the few people that lurk in corners avert their eyes, studiously ignoring the little car.

Müller is there behind the big desk, with the Hauptmann standing beside him looking embarrassed. Le Clerq is made to stand facing the major, waiting while he reads a two-page document before looking up. 'Well, priest. Are we to assume that you are no longer following your calling?' He studies the curé with a cold expression.

'I am without a church.'

'Not a congregation though, surely?' Müller leans forward with a sardonic twist to his mouth. 'Are you telling me you need stone and timber to preach to your flock? I thought religion went deeper than that.'

'I need time to think.'

The major raps a staccato on the desk-top with his pencil. 'Time is a luxury at the moment, priest. We must all have a purpose now, for it is a time of crisis. I ask again. Are you a priest, or are you not?'

'You destroyed my church. I need to adjust, then I will seek advice from my superiors.'

'Perhaps I do not make myself clear, priest.' The Hauptmann translates word for word, his voice cold as stone, but Le Clerq never takes his eyes from Müller's cruel face. 'You are a man without a duty, and in these times everyone must have a duty if we are to make Europe a better place. You will be enlisted in the STO and play your part in the making of a new world. You will have time to consult your conscience while you work.'

Le Clerq holds his face deadpan. The Service de Travail Obligatoire is detested throughout France. Over a million of his countrymen, along with Poles, Russians, Dutch, Belgians and others are working in German factories, mostly against their will. Now, it seems, he is about to join them. 'I must protest – I am still the curé.'

The pencil is slapped hard on the desk. 'I see only a civilian. There is no argument. You will stay here in the village until we know where you are to be sent. Do not attempt to leave, Le Clerq. Such an act will be regarded as treason, and you will be shot. Do not try my patience any more.' He turns to the sergeant standing at the curé's side. 'Take him away and put him with the others.'

The light is fading, and the shadows of the village are deeper as he is led to the small schoolhouse, where he finds several other grim-faced men awaiting the same fate. They look up for a moment when he enters the class-room, then withdraw into themselves and there is an air of hopelessness about them.

Three

Cyclops is back at sea again after an extended working-up period, following a series of problems with mains engines, aircraft lifts and other essential equipment. She has spent many days in harbour or swinging round buoys in remote Scottish backwaters while relations between the ship's company and squadron personnel grow steadily worse, and the co-operation that should exist to make her an efficient fighting unit is lacking. Now she steadies her bow upwind into a blustering sea and prepares to refuel her brood of thirsty destroyers, who will come alongside to suckle one by one during the forenoon. During the time it takes to complete the evolution they will be vulnerable, so everyone is anxious to get it done quickly and efficiently.

Mort is in charge of a party of seamen making preparations to pass the big hose across with the aid of the crane situated just abaft the 'island'. They are in the confined area of the main deck that is tucked in beneath the overhanging gun-sponsons and it is like working in a large shop-window without the glass. Like every other deck job in an aircraft-carrier it has to be done in a restrictive, closed-in environment, and men have to lean out of alcoves to see what goes on forward or aft. Seamen like him, who are used to the open expanse of a fo'c'sle, or the upper deck of a conventional ship where heaving lines can be thrown with gay abandon, and hawsers manhandled from one set of fairleads to another without needing to be passed outboard of large chunks of the ship's side, are still having difficulty finding ways to get round the obstacles.

Petty Officer Envoldsen is on the flight-deck, ready to send a thin coston-gun line snaking across to the destroyer when she hauls up alongside, so that the all-important distance-line can be stretched between the two ships to monitor their positions throughout the transfer. Once that is accomplished the heavier ropes can be hauled over, with the weight of the fuel-pipe itself taken by the crane. When the bight is lowered, Mort and his gang must grab the end of the hose and drag it into their small cavern, so that stokers can couple it up for pumping. While this goes on the destroyermen will attach the hose to their end. It is an exacting task, with much of the onus placed on the skills of the two men at the helms, who must hold their ships on a steady course.

As the destroyer creeps into position from astern of the carrier, her wash meets that of the twenty-four thousand ton hull of *Cyclops*, to converge in a turmoil of white-crested confusion between them. She plunges her sleek bow into the on-coming swells before lifting clear with foam and spray spewing out over her scuppers. She shows the red-lead of her bilges as far aft as 'A' gun when she rides over the crests, and men gathered on the raised gun-deck just forward of her bridge get deluged time and time again as they wait for the line to reach them. Both ships bluster on as though they are on parallel rails as inch by inch the destroyer brings herself abreast. Envoldsen's .303 sends the thin line arcing across to fall into the grasping hands, and the work begins. The carrier maintains her speed while the destroyer adjusts her revolutions until they surge on side by side as though joined by an invisible union.

In the tiny wheelhouse far below the bridge in the protective belt of armour Wally stares with hypnotic eyes into the oblong gyro-repeater while his hands caress the small, wooden-spoked wheel to keep the ship's head within half a degree either side of the ordered course. This is his forte: the little round man has been acknowledged the best helmsman in the ship, and this is his action station, his special sea duty station. He has built up an affinity with the huge ship. Discovered how she responds to sea conditions, speed and the influence of wind on her huge freeboard. He knows exactly the moment to check her before she starts to swing her ponderous bows off-course. He is in tune with her, and can anticipate the tricks she would like to play on him. The two telegraphmen standing each side of him have learned to remain silent while he responds to every command from the voice-pipe, and the door leading out into the passage is firmly closed to shut them off from the outside world. Nothing will distract Wally's concentration.

Another man might have panicked when he felt an unusual slackness in the wheel and caught the hesitation on the helm indicator. Not Wally; his level tone betrays nothing of the surge of anxiety that runs through his body when he reports a possible malfunction in the steering gear. There are moments of grace before the ship realises she is off the leash. Time for an alert captain to use his engines to counter her swing, but the first priority is to get both ships clear of each other. The emergency order is passed over the RT to the destroyer's captain who reacts immediately. Too immediately. He could have held on a few vital seconds for the hose to be disconnected. As it is his one desire is to get his fragile little ship clear of the huge flank of the aircraft carrier.

'Cast off the fuel-pipe!' he yells to his number one, who urges the stokers to move quickly. Sensing impending disaster they fumble the job while the order to put the helm over sets the wheel spinning, and the bow begins to swing away. The big, looping bight begins to flatten out and the pipe itself slides through the cradles. Soon it is stretched taut between the two ships, and before the pump can be stopped the hose is torn from its coupling to disgorge thick fuel-oil over them all and fill the area with its glutinous mess. As though this is not enough, the loose end swings wildly in the cradle and wraps round the hook and wire of the crane. Unable to release it the flight-deck party watch transfixed as the jib is yanked viciously over to one side, and the wire jumps out of its pulley to rip through part of the metal frame-work.

'Shit!' growls the commander uncharacteristically, as he sees his one crane put out of action.

'Small beer,' comforts the captain. 'We can live without a crane.' He resumes his seat philosophically. Nothing less than a major disaster will persuade him to return to port. The minor steering fault that caused the panic has been repaired, and there is no reason why they cannot fuel their destroyers in the old-fashioned way: with the fuel-pipe led out over the stern.

Petty Officer Envoldsen stands on the quarterdeck where canvas is stretched across the bleached wooden deck to save its sanctified surface from becoming blemished. He glowers at the stokers. 'If so much as one pint of that muck gets onto my paintwork I will personally dangle yer over the side by your bollocks while yer cleans it orf. We've already 'ad one cock-up due to the clumsy bastard of a birdman who was too bloody slow on the crane.'

That is the version carried down into the messdecks by the seamen and the blame for the accident is set squarely in the airside's corner. Not to be outdone the airmen apportion the blame firmly in the other court with the helmsman as their prime culprit. The argument rages to and fro, and the rift between both sides becomes even wider.

Mort and his men are ordered below to scrub away the cloying filth from their bodies. The thick oil has a certain amount of acidity in its make-up which has ruined their clothing, and is already inflaming the soft part of their skin. The leading hand strips off quickly to his underwear and grabs his dhobi bucket, only to find young Wordsley standing beside him, naked except for a towel round his waist.

'What's up with you?' asks Mort gruffly.

The OD points to the bucket. 'Where did you get a chromium-plated bucket like that?'

'That, me old son,' says Mort proudly, holding it up for inspection, 'is an ordinary galvanised bucket.' He reaches into his locker and produces a small leather square faced with what looks like chain-mail. 'You take this burnishing pad and about ten tins of metal-polish, and you sweats your guts out rubbing away the rough dullness until it shines like this. Every matelot needs a good dhobi bucket, laddy. There ain't no laundries in pusser ships, and with one of these you can do your washing anywhere, even on the upper deck if the weather's right. I always say that all you need to make life bearable in this man's Navy is a clean set of underwear. Now,' he adds, changing the subject, 'if you're gonna scrub that lot off you before they call us to action stations or something, you'd better get cracking.' He leads the way through the bulkhead door, straight to the galley where he cadges a bucket of steaming hot water before heading for the bathroom. Other men are cursing the tepid water in the so-called hot taps.

Wordsley hardly takes his eyes off Mort as he stirs a handful of soap chippings into the water until it lathers up nicely. Most other men have scrubbed down and drifted away, content to let the Navy replace their soiled underwear, but the leading hand prizes his shop-bought kit too much to throw it away needlessly.

'Where do you get the soap-flakes, Hooky?'

Mort is getting tired of questions. It's like having a five-year-old hanging about persistently asking 'why'. However, he is conscious of his responsibilities as a leading hand and explains patiently. 'They ain't soapflakes, laddy. They are shavings from a bar of 'pusser's hard.' He picks up a chunk of solid yellow Naval issue soap. 'You can't work up a lather with rubbish like this, so you gets your knife and shaves off enough to make a lather.'

There are only a few men in the bathroom now, and the two men are standing close together in the corner entirely nude when Malloy pokes his head through the door. 'Don't take too long over that. You must be back at your defence stations in ten minutes.' He starts to leave then spots the two of them in the corner. 'Well now, what 'ave we 'ere?' He steps over the coaming into the steamy compartment, wading through an inch or so of scummy water until he stands close to the naked men. 'What's this then, Hooky? Got yerself a little winger?'

'Piss off, Malloy. Don't be so fucking stupid.'

The other man's eyes flash dangerously, but his taunting smile stays set. 'No need ter worry. I'm not the sort to break up a romance.' He backs off with a laugh when Mort advances angrily. 'Man born of man shall live forever, eh, Mort?' he scoffs from the door with a harsh laugh before disappearing. Several pairs of eyes hastily turn away from Mort's glare. He gathers up his gear and wraps a towel round his waist before noticing Wordsley still standing naked, his pale skin shining wet. 'He's an idiot, but he's right. You'd better get a move on,' he growls, and moves out into the passage.

*

As *Cyclops* and her escorts steam out into the Western Approaches they run into the teeth of a deep depression sweeping in from mid-Atlantic, with winds gusting to eighty miles an hour. Soon the destroyers are forced to reduce speed until they are virtually hove-to. Even so, they are being hammered by green seas that smash inboard as far aft as their bridges, so that the forward guns and anti-submarine weapons have to be abandoned. It makes small odds, for the enemy is equally affected, and kept impotent by the huge swells as the elements take over and render the weak efforts of men to wage war futile.

All the escorts can do is batten down and ride it out while they count the cost as boats are smashed to matchwood, carley rafts torn from their fixings and broken crockery mixes with a swirl of filthy sea-water and vomit in the mess-decks. One destroyer broaches to and disappears from view for long, agonising minutes until it recovers and lifts onto the crest of a swell with its funnel buckled to look like a broken fag-end. On the carrier's bridge they hold their breath as they watch her pivot with white water spewing from her upper-deck until she crashes down into a steep dive that buries her bow into a solid wall of ocean; then she rides clear once again, fighting back to an even keel as she is brought under control once more. There is a change in her appearance which puzzles them until they realise that she has rolled one of her guns clean out of its mounting.

On *Cyclops* the flight deck is put out of bounds as she digs her big, square bows into monstrous swells, and the wind hurls solid bodies of ocean across the expanse of the exposed deck. All aircraft are struck down into the hangar, and a modified version of defence stations is introduced, whereby only a token number of gun crews are closed up while the threat of an air attack is almost non-existent. Malloy is in charge of the twin bofors on the port sponson opposite the 'island', and his crew attempt to escape the worst of the storm by huddling into a corner under the forward end with the extended lead of the headphones stretched almost to breaking point from the mounting. The picture they stare out at is of a bleak wilderness of huge, grey seas heaving by beneath a lowering canopy of heavy cloud. Squalls of driving rain accompany the violent gusts of wind howling through the radio mast just above their position. They are wet, cold and miserable. To carry on any sort of conversation is impossible because every word needs to be shouted above the storm, and in any case Malloy's intolerant manner does not allow for normal repartee. His is a solemn regime where junior ratings are discouraged from making comment and seniors withdraw into themselves rather than incur the snide comments that over-rides any effort to inject an air of matiness into the situation.

Now he sits brooding on an ammunition locker, wallowing in self-pity as he glowers at the miserable waste of tormented sea. Layer by layer his status has been stripped from him until he has no prestige at all, and has been made to look an idiot on several occasions by Mort. He has not been able to gather a bunch of toadies about him like he did in barracks, and the tight four-hour-on, four-hour-off routine with frequent calls to action stations leaves no time to organise any rackets or swindles that could have added a little spice to his grotty existence. Somehow he must find a way to get his own back, and that idea dominates all his waking hours.

The Supply Officer is alive to conditions on the guns and other exposed positions and orders the cooks to boil up a rich soup which can be taken to those on duty to feed life back into their cold bodies. It falls to Wordsley to negotiate the heaving decks and reeling ladders that seem determined to hurl him and his mess-kettle into a messy heap. After a great deal of painful effort he staggers into Malloy's sponson with hardly a drop spilled, to be welcomed with shouts of gratitude as they drag out mugs from remote corners to receive their share of steaming hot measures of fragrant soup as it is ladled out by the grinning youngster. Finally he is confronted by Malloy who stands over him with glowering hatred in his face.

'What the hell do yer think you're doin'?'

Taken aback the smile freezes and Wordsley looks about him for assurance, but the crew are silent now, turning away with their mugs, unwilling to become involved. The wind growls menacingly as Wordsley peers uncertainly into his mess-kettle.

'I've brought some soup, Hooky,' he explains lamely. 'There's plenty here if you've got your mug.'

'You slimy little bastard! Don't yer know enough ter report ter the captain of the gun before yer starts dishin' aht soup ter the crew? I get the fuckin' dregs, do I?'

'I'm sorry, Hooky. I – I didn't think. They ain't just dregs though,' he adds eagerly. 'There's enough for two wacks for everybody.'

'I don't want anythin' that's bin mucked abaht by a poncy little brahn-hatter like you, you filthy sod – go back to yer sugar-daddy and feed 'im yer muck; don't bring it ter me. It'll make me puke.' He kicks the kettle out of the startled youngster's hands to send it flying into the air, where it is caught by the wind and hurled into the flight-deck, and rolls across the surface until it catches in one of the arrester wires. Almost without thinking, Wordsley climbs the short ladder to peer over the edge of the deck to see it wedged under the slack wire. One of the crew grabs his legs. 'Come dahn out of it. You'll get yoursen killed, for Christ's sake!'

'It's still there, caught in the wire,' blurts the lad.

'Well it can bleedin' well stay there. It ain't worth riskin' your neck for. Anyway, no one is allowed on the flight deck.'

'Only if they're ordered ter go,' states Malloy. 'I ain't gonna pay fer no bloody mess-kettle. You'd better fetch it back, Wordsley.'

The AB is still holding on to the lad. 'It's bloody suicide to go up there, Malloy. Anyway you ain't got the authority to make him go.'

'I'll go.' Wordsley snaps the words out, staring defiantly into Malloy's face. 'I'll get the soddin' thing back – I wouldn't want you to lose out, Malloy.'

'Don't be an idiot,' snarls the AB.

'Shut yer mouth,' barks Malloy. 'Get that kettle, or I'll put you in the rattle fer losin' government property.'

The OD climbs the ladder and takes a precautionary look over the edge. Clouds of spray sweep across the expanse of wet flight-deck, but the wind seems to have eased a little, and in any case there is a safety net running the length of the ship on either side, so even if the wind is too strong he can lie flat and work his way across into one of them. The best thing to do is use one of the lowered crash-barriers to work his way to the centre so that he is directly in front of the kettle before crawling back until he can grasp the arrester wire. After that it should be easy to haul himself to one side, and into one of the sponsons. He can see no reason why he should not retrieve the kettle quite easily.

*

In his small compartment Mort is fiddling with his controls in an effort to obtain a reasonable picture amongst all the mess of false echoes thrown back by the huge waves. His eyes are aching with concentration, but he has to concede that the set is useless in these conditions. He reports as much to the man in the ADR only to be told to remain at his station until things improve. He sighs, throws his chinograph pencil onto the table in disgust and leans back in his chair with his fingers intertwined behind his head. A gust of wind stronger than average howls past his scuttle and he goes to peer out at the storm.

When he opens the deadlight and sticks his head out the

wind blasts into his face as though it is a solid mass. The air is full of stinging spray flying horizontally past the opening. Staring squint-eyed into it he can just see the big, square bow plunging down towards a huge body of water that blots out the horizon and lifts to crouch over her like a monstrous beast with a spuming crest edging the black sky. Despite the cruel needles lancing into his eyes he is compelled to watch as she smashes into the wave with a force that sends a shudder through the ship. She buries her head into its mass, and a massive explosion of white surf heaves up to be snatched by the wind and hurled aft along the length of the sloping deck. He has to turn away then, to pull his head in before the solid body of ocean reaches the 'island', and it is then that he sees Wordsley midway across the deck, gripping hard to the crash-barrier and staring with horrified eyes into the wall of water about to descend on him.

Mort watches transfixed while the wave washes over the prostrate body. The youngster buries his head in his arms and hangs on desperately against the lifting pull of the wave until it subsides to leave him drenched and unable to move. The bow lifts now, cutting out some of the wind, and hands are reaching under his armpits, hauling him clear, and forcing his clutching fingers to release their grip. He is dragged into the blessed warmth and security of the island and the door is rammed back into place against the pressure of the wind. Only then is it possible to communicate. The leading hand pushes Wordsley into the radar cabin.

'What the bloody hell do you think you're doing, you silly little sod?'

'Trying to get the mess-kettle back. It's jammed in one of the arrester wires.'

Mort is still trying to work that one out when the door bursts open and a PO from the ADR bursts in. 'Your phone must be out of order,' he begins, then sees the sodden state they are in. 'Jesus! What goes on here? What's he doing here?' he demands.

The youngster's teeth are chattering. 'I – I got caught by a

big wave. Hooky helped me to get to shelter.'
'Helped you from where?'
'All right, kid,' says Mort quietly. 'Leave it to me.' He turns
to the PO. 'He was trying to get hold of a mess-kettle before it
went over the side is my guess, and got caught by that big wave
that smashed over the flight deck. I nipped out the door and
dragged him back inside. He was just outside – it wasn't any
real problem.'
The PO's face hardens. 'What was he doing out there in the
first place? It's out of bounds.'
In the gun-sponson the impact of the huge wave sends the
guncrew diving for cover before the overflow pours into the
mounting. They feel the heavy thump as the bow smashes into
the swell, and one of the ABs spits out the time-honoured
'another bloody milestone' as *Cyclops* staggers in her effort to
regain an even keel. The bulk of the wave passes down the
ship's side, and at one time the crest is almost level with the
sponson as she rolls into it. It is a freak wave that grew out of
the combination of several conflicting forces to peak right in
the path of the carrier. Once past it dies to merge with the
convulsions of the storm and when it is gone they begin to
recover and remember the OD. Someone clambers up the
ladder to see the whole expanse of flight deck swept clean with
the dregs of the wave still running over the sides. The
mess-kettle is gone, and there is no sign of life. 'Bloody hell!'
he gasps. ''E's gorn!'
'Gone!' growls Malloy aggressively. 'What d'yer mean –
gone?'
'What I say. He ain't there any more. Nor is the mess-kettle.
They've both disappeared.'
'That don't mean 'e's gone over the side,' states Malloy
without any real conviction.
'Like shit it doesn't!' The AB grabs the telephone on the
bulk-head that connects them with the bridge and twirls the
handle vigorously. 'Number four bofors here, sir. There's a
man overboard.'
Cyclops' siren blares, and a string of signal flags hoists up to

her yardarm. The twenty-one inch lamp on the nearest destroyer begins to blink an offer to come round and go in search. An offer that is immediately turned down by the carrier's captain as his imagination conjures up a vivid picture of the fragile little ship broadside to the ranks of massive swell running down from ahead. The likelihood of anyone surviving for more than a few moments in that turbulence is non-existent and he won't risk lives in a fruitless quest. Nevertheless an effort must be made, even if it is only a token one.

'Get as many volunteers as you can to back up the lookouts,' he orders, then turns to the Officer of the Watch. 'Now let's see how well she behaves broadside on to this lot.'

'D'ye hear there!' shouts the tannoy. 'The ship is about to turn. Secure all gear in the messdecks, and stand by for heavy rolling. Off-duty volunteers are required for lookout – there is a man overboard.'

In Mort's radar cabin he and the PO exchange looks then focus on the bedraggled heap in the corner and leap to the same conclusion. The leading hand grabs his microphone to call up the ADR. His message is relayed to the bridge as *Cyclops* takes her first broadside and rolls over to an angle that sends loose gear crashing down the slope of her decks. Men hang on desperately: waiting for her to right herself, but she hangs there with every guy and coupling straining to keep aircraft and heavy gear from breaking free, then, unbelievably, she lists even further as another swell reaches her before she can recover. In the hangar a towing vehicle hurtles through the closely packed aircraft and brings up sharp against the ship's side where handlers struggle to secure it with ropes. Men and equipment tumble in confusion, and it is a miracle that no one is seriously hurt. Throughout the ship there is a bedlam of sound as crockery spills from lockers and mess gear scatters all over the place. At last, with everyone holding his breath she heaves back onto an even keel, hesitates, then sends the whole sorry mess tumbling in the opposite direction when she rolls to starboard.

The carrier is well into her swing to port when Mort's message reaches the bridge, so it is too late to stop the turn, and she has to go on with it until she is stern-to the sea. Once settled on that course things become much more stable. The following wind loses a lot of its strength, and the sea is less violent, even though the helmsman finds his task difficult just to keep her from broaching to. The unfortunate part of it all is that the escorts and carrier are now on opposite courses, with no immediate prospect of turning, so the distance between them grows wider with every minute.

Damage reports are coming in from all parts of the ship telling of masses of broken crockery and minor injuries. A cook has been scalded by steam while trying to negotiate a course through the galley when the deck was awash with spilled soup and islands of meat and veg. The most serious damage is to aircraft in the hangar where the towing vehicle went berserk and rampaged through the area. While deep down in the bowels of the ship a quantity of bofors ammunition is strewn about a magazine from broken metal containers, every round live, and just waiting for a sharp corner to come into contact with a percussion cap. The list grows until the captain decides the situation is serious enough to warrant returning to harbour for repairs.

While he is in the process of composing a signal to that effect a coded message from the Admiralty arrives which orders them to steam to an area of the English Channel and send off strikes against several targets on the Cotentin Peninsula and the Normandy coast. The targets include the airfield near the road leading from Cherbourg to Barfleur, military traffic on that road and, in particular, a new radar installation located on the headland north of Caen.

It takes forty-eight hours for the weather to abate and allow the group to reform in preparation to close in towards the French coast. During that time the ship's company work round the clock to clear up the mess and get their ship into fighting trim, while several wrecked aircraft are brought up from the hangar and ditched overside. By dawn of the third day eighteen aircraft are ranged on the flight-deck. Eight Avengers will attack the airfield, each carrying four five hundred pound bombs and escorted by four Corsairs: while four other Corsairs with two bombs beneath their wing-roots will go for the radar station. The remaining two Corsairs will fly a carrier air patrol above the small fleet.

Lieutenant-Commander Potter moves out with other shadowy figures to climb into his cockpit. The crimson sunrise outlines the black shapes of the aircraft sharply and the men work silently as the pilots strap on their harness, adjust their helmets and goggles, and connect RT leads and oxygen pipes. *Cyclops* is swinging her bulk into the wind once more, with one of the destroyers taking up station off her starboard quarter. He runs through his check-list. Magneto, control locks, rudder, elevator, ailerons. One by one he checks until he is satisfied, ready with the propeller at full-fine pitch and the mixture control to full rich with the cowling gills on the big Pratt and Whitney open.

The petrol cock on the main self-sealing tank between him and the engine is open. The fitter acknowledges his 'thumbs up' and gives the propeller a couple of turns against compression, then stands well back while Topper switches on the master-switch. A couple of squirts of neat fuel into the cylinders and a final check with the fitter that all is clear before switching on the magneto and pressing the starter-button. One by one the Koffman starters ignite with heavy, asthmatic coughs and the engines backfire before shattering the morning with their concerted roar. At five hundred revs he waits for the oil-pressure to settle on 'normal', then opens the throttle to one thousand revs to check both magnetos. He throttles back and crosses his hands in front of his face.

Once again he gets the 'thumbs up' and responds to the first marshal who is already waving him on. The Corsair bounces over the crash-barriers as he taxies towards the catapult. Out of sight beneath him the strop is attached and he closes the gills and locks the seat harness, bracing back as the tailwheel is locked. He gets the signal to open the throttle wide. At two thousand four hundred revs the little flag is revolving for the final vital few seconds before it slaps down and the seat hits him in the back as the Corsair leaps forward to clear the deck. He holds her down for a few seconds, feeling the power lifting the aircraft against him, before pulling her up in a wide, climbing turn to port. The exhilaration is there as always at this moment when a glance over his left shoulder shows *Cyclops* creaming through the ruffled ocean with her aircraft lining up to take their turn on the catapult. He throttles back to wait for the others to form up on him, and soon they are taking departure to settle on course, flying into the sunrise on the first full-scale mission since *Cyclops* was commissioned.

Meanwhile the carrier resumes her routine, and at 0930 the captain holds his 'table', with a motley crowd of requestmen and defaulters lined up for judgement. Malloy is there, standing last in the queue with eyes focused on the deck while he waits. At last the Master-at-Arms barks, and he doubles up to the table and removes his cap to stare straight into space while the charge is read out. One by one the witnesses are called to give their versions of the events that show clearly that he was responsible for sending Wordsley out onto the flight deck in direct disobedience of an order.

A blind man could sense the animosity amongst the gun's crew when they testify, and when his Divisional Officer makes no effort to put forward any redeeming commendations, but goes out of his way to stress Malloy's abysmal record, the captain has no hesitation in passing sentence. Malloy loses his 'hook' and becomes an able seaman once more. To save embarrassment he is moved out of his mess and finds himself carrying out the duties of messman to the artificers when he is not closed up at action stations. To a man who has always been top dog amongst his associates the ignomony of washing dishes, serving meals, and cleaning up after others festers inside like a malignant growth.

Chief Ordinance Artificer Hughes is a fastidious man with little common sense, and even less diplomacy. The other chiefs and POs of the mess do not encroach on the tiny world of their messmen, respecting the small amount of privacy they have in their pantry where they spend all their off-duty hours. Hughes is the exception.

Malloy is on his own when Hughes decides to enter the pantry to ask for a cup of tea. The gun-layer makes no secret of his annoyance. 'I'll pass it out ter yer, chief. If yer go back inter the mess.'

The chief edges past, sidling along the narrow space between the lockers that line each bulkhead. He is inspecting everything: running fingers over the paintwork and tut-tutting at the small ridge of dust that shows on his wet skin. At the far end there is a small stack of dishes waiting to be washed. He swirls a hand in the hot water.

'There's no soap in this water,' he accuses.

Malloy is measuring scoops of tea into the strainer before inserting it into the mess fanny. He makes no reply as he takes it across to the steaming boiler beside the serving hatch, opens the cock and allows the boiling water to pour over the tea. When it is full he knocks the tap closed with the heel of his hand in quick jabs, for the tap is too hot to handle.

Hughes turns and glares at him. 'Did you hear what I said? I arranged especially for adequate supplies of soap. It is un-hygienic to wash dirty dishes without soap. I had cause to reprimand your predecessor for the same reason.' His high-pitched voice rambles on, grating on Malloy's nerves. 'You have got soap, haven't you?'

'Yes, chief, I have got some soap.' The tone is level, ominous to anyone with normal sensitivity.

'I thought so. I went to great lengths to obtain it, Malloy. Where is it? I will put some in myself.' He starts opening locker doors, then slamming them shut again, muttering all the time.

Malloy is shaking now, his lips tight as he speaks through clenched teeth. 'There's only a couple of cups and saucers – I was gonna rinse them out in fresh water to save on soap.'

'You should always use soap – give it to me.'

'I said I'd do it, chief.' Malloy is breathing hard. 'If yer go back into the mess, I'll do it.'

'I want to see it done. Where's the – '

The tea fanny hits him full in the face and scalding water drenches his shoulders and upper body. He screams in agony as Malloy dives at him, swinging the fanny at him again and again. Men come running into the pantry, and the wild-eyed gunlayer has to be dragged away from his victim, fighting all the time. It takes half a dozen marines to manhandle him forward to the cells where he is stripped of his bootlaces and other items that might be used to do himself injury before being thrown into an empty cell. He is the first man to be confined in the wretched, spartan punishment compartment right up in the eye of the ship.

Four

Nicole wakes with a start, staring into the shadows of a strange room while she strives to recall why she is here on this couch, listening to the farmyard noises as pale light filters through the cottage window. The sound seems to grow with the light. There are secret mutterings and squeakings all about the place and, above all, the human noises from beyond the plain wooden door that leads to a bedroom. She can hear snoring and it makes her angry to think of Camille lying beside her soldier – 'soldier' – what a name for that scared youngster from Strasbourg who cannot make up his mind whether he is French or German, and tries to forget the death sentence that hangs over him while he is in Camille's soft arms.

She found them together yesterday. Frightened and lonely. Anxious to make her understand that they have found something more important than war to live for. They are going to hide here until it is all over. Waiting for the fighting to wash over them and fade away in the distance like an ebbing tide so that they can build a new life together. She laughed ironically at them for their naivety, even though deep down she felt a twinge of sympathy. They are like children, believing the world will turn from slaughter to smile on them. It is pathetic.

'What do you think will happen to you when we are liberated?' she taunted Camille. 'What do you think will happen to all those like you who went with the Germans?' She turned and slated the boy. 'And you. Now that you see which way the wind blows you suddenly remember how French you are. There are many like you, and they are all going to get what's coming to them.'

Camille had pouted, on the verge of tears. 'Mathias says they will never land here; everyone knows that.'

Nicole did not even bother to argue with them. They are too stupid to understand what is going on. She had waited with them for Le Clerq to return, then, when he did not come back and it grew dark, she decided to remain overnight rather than risk being caught out after curfew. Now she is anxious about him. He is the only man in the village she can fully trust.

She gets up from the couch to bathe her face with cold water from the big jug near the sink. In the small, cracked mirror her face is tanned and her eyes deep brown beneath dark brows. 'Gypsylike' her mother says, and there is a wildness in her that erupts at times. Yet there is also a softness that she tries to hide, even from herself: but it is there all right, and when she sees the way these two love-birds look at each other and talk of the Utopia they will never find, she feels a surge of compassion.

The wind that rattled the eaves last night has died away, and when she steps outside the world is waking to a fine day. She disturbs a small herd of cattle lying grouped together in the corner of a meadow, and they stare at her with big solemn eyes before scrambling up to stretch their bodies while steam rises from their flanks; then they arch their backs to defecate before moving off to find fresh pasture. Already the sun is warm on her face and it is impossible not to feel a sense of well-being on such a perfect day.

A new sound swings her round to see Mathias staring at her from the doorway. He wears loose peasant clothes, and a blue cotton cap with a large peak to shadow his pale face. He makes a pathetic figure, and she wonders what Camille can see in him.

'You had better stay indoors,' she says bluntly.

'I know, but I have something I wish to tell you.' His eyes are searching hers, full of anxiety; almost pleading. 'It will help you to understand that I am genuine.'

She looks away. She would like to tell him to go to hell, but something in his tone arouses her curiosity, so without answering, she follows him inside where Camille watches her with big, beseeching eyes. They must have whispered together throughout the night and come to a decision in the warmth of the bed, and now Nicole is to be told her part in their conspiracy. He looks so immature with his thin, pale face, yet if this is the same man that she saw with Camille that night four years ago he must be in his twenties. She looks at Camille's foolish face and wonders how many Mathiases there have been.

'It is about the radar station.' She jerks back from her thoughts. The strange texture of his French is almost like a foreign accent to a Norman.

'Radar station?'

He crouches forward with his hands clasped on the table, eager to gain her complete attention. 'It is not a real one. The one they have set up where the church was, I mean. There is nothing there, no wires, no instruments, nothing.'

She shrugs. 'So they have not completed it yet. Why should that be important?'

He shakes his head impatiently. 'No. You do not understand. The real station is on top of the cliffs, near the pine-trees, and they have made it look like part of the scenery. All the workings are there and the Navy operators live in some outbuildings. The aerial they put up at the ruins of the church is a sham.'

She shrugs dismissively. 'So why tell me? What do you think I can do about it?'

Camille comes forward. 'You know the resistance, Nicole. Mathias would like to join them. He worked up there with the Todt – guarding some of the foreign slaves and he knows all there is to know about where the installations are.'

'Nicole,' he urges, 'in my unit there are French, Poles, even Russians. They wear German uniforms, but most of them are sick of it all like me. Especially when we find ourselves guarding some of our own countrymen. Now that the SS have come it will get worse.'

'I can promise nothing,' she says coldly. 'Why you think I am in touch with the Maquisard I do not know, but I will talk to the curé when I find him, and see what he has to say. Until then you are on your own.' She looks hard at Mathias. 'There might be some excuse for you, being born in Alsace: I know there was conscription there, but these others you speak of are traitors – remember that.' She rises, prepared to leave.

Camille comes to her, a kind of panic in her face as she holds on to Nicole and pleads. 'You will come back to us, Nicole?' The tears course down her plump cheeks. 'We are so alone.'

Nicole wrenches away without another word, angry because she is choked and feels another surge of compassion welling up inside. She knows they are standing in the doorway watching with their arms round each other as she goes up the cart-track, but she will not look back at them. Damn them both for making her feel this way. She hurries along, as though each step takes her back to sanity.

She gets no further than the end of the track before she glimpses a vehicle far down the road, just before it dips out of sight in the valley. She can hear the engine struggle as it climbs the winding hill that leads up to the farm. She spins round; running towards the cottage, yelling and waving her arms. Mathias appears at the door, takes one look and races towards the barn. Camille is slow to react, and stands gazing about incredulously. Nicole has to push her roughly inside. 'Stay with me. They might be bringing Father Le Clerq. Anyway, it is better we stay clear of Mathias.'

The army lorry scatters hens and geese in all directions as it bumps down the track and rumbles to a halt in front of the cottage. Soldiers pile out to run off in pairs and begin searching the area, while a sergeant and two men approach Nicole who waits at the door to meet them.

'I come to search the house,' the sergeant states in poor French. 'We are looking for a deserter.' He is a sober, weather-beaten man with greying eyebrows, and she can see he is one of the Hauptmann's soldiers which makes her feel easier. He notices Camille standing behind in the shadows, scared, anxious and staring about her as though she would like to run away, but he says nothing as his men push past into the room. Before they can start a yell comes from the barn and two soldiers emerge with the wretched figure of Mathias between them. Camille gives a stifled scream with her fists pressed in hard against her mouth.

'Stay here!' the sergeant warns Nicole. 'Do not get involved.' He orders his men into the lorry and it jerks into motion with Mathias staring back at them with haunted eyes. Nicole keeps Camille in the shadows where she whimpers miserably, her body shaking as she stares after him. The lorry backs up to make its turn and stops with its motor idling as a small half-track drives down the lane. Nicole recognises Major Müller seated beside the driver. The SS make the Hauptmann's troops look scruffy, for there is a brisk military arrogance in the way they go about their business. Müller ignores the sergeant as he strides to the rear of the truck and orders the garrison soldiers to dismount, along with their prisoner.

Nicole has seen enough, and turns to push Camille inside when Müller's '*Halt!*' freezes her. She looks back as he and the sergeant march across. The sergeant interprets with difficulty, needing to plan his phrases before speaking. 'The major wishes to know how many other deserters the priest is hiding in his house?'

'This has nothing to do with the curé.'

Müller laughs contemptuously and makes a sneering comment, nodding in Nicole's direction without deigning to look at her as he fires sharp questions at the sergeant. The replies come quickly enough, but they do not satisfy the major, and he delivers a tirade that has the NCO wilting as he stands rigidly at attention. The SS have Mathias now, and bundle him into the half-track while the blank-faced infantrymen line up alongside their truck. The major knows full well he has no right to interfere in the Wehrmacht's affairs, but there is no one here with courage enough to object, and the sergeant is reduced to acting as interpreter.

'Do you live here?' he asks Nicole.

She catches the warning look in his eye. 'No,' she replies quickly. 'I came to visit my friend.' She points to Camille's distraught figure. 'I stayed overnight because otherwise I would have missed curfew.' At last the major seems satisfied that there is nothing more to be gained. Nevertheless as the men climb into their vehicles he turns and raps out a sneering command. The sergeant salutes and delivers a final sally. 'The major says he is no fool. The girl will be punished enough. Next time she should choose a soldier and not a weak-minded peasant.'

When the sound of the engines has died Nicole clasps Camille's shoulders in a strong grip and talks earnestly to her. 'You must go to the village and try to act as though nothing has happened.' The girl starts to blubber uncontrollably and she shakes her viciously. 'Do as I say,' she snaps angrily. 'I have things to do.'

The distant sound of gunfire comes in on the wind as she closes the door. It is the quick, rhythmic percussion of light anit-aircraft guns and she looks up at the sky. There has been no warning, but the siren doesn't reach here when the wind blows from the west so that means nothing. She pushes Camille on her way and sets off down the little lane that meets the main road to Caen further south. If she hurries she will catch Marcel as he sets out for his first load. The guns are heavier now, reverberating on the air like thunder, and there is the sound of aircraft like angry bees in the distance. They must be small 'planes, she thinks to herself. Not the heavy bombers that have been carrying out high-level attacks on airfields and railway junctions recently. She presses on towards the main road while the deep crump of bombs punctuates the chatter of the guns. Whatever the target, it is not close enough to disrupt the traffic on the Caen road.

Near the end of the lane is a small lay-by, and she decides to wait there. Nearly all the traffic is military so Marcel's faded red cab is easy to spot as it comes into view, and she steps out to the verge to wave him down. As always he is full of himself, leaning right out of his window as he toots his horn and grins at her. She steels herself to put up with his stupid banter and explains why she is there. Eventually he runs out of steam and becomes more serious.

'Not another of your mad schemes, Nicole,' he accuses. 'The Colonel doesn't trust you too much. It isn't a game we are playing, you know.'

She bristles. 'If talk could win wars, Marcel, it would have all been over a long time ago. I want to see the Colonel. You must know where he is.'

Before he has time to reply their attention is caught by a small aircraft that lifts out of the valley between them and the village. Its engine is losing power, coughing and spluttering until it reaches the top of its climb, hovers for a moment, then stalls into a steep dive towards a copse a couple of kilometres from the road. The white canopy of a parachute blossoms and is caught by the wind to be driven towards the east.

'Get in the lorry,' snaps Marcel sharply. 'We must reach that flier before the Germans do. I think I know where he is coming down.'

Whatever else she thinks of Marcel, she has to admire the way he drives his huge lorry through the narrow, winding lanes. As he negotiates the twists and turns he laughs. 'You wanted to see the Colonel? Well, if I'm not mistaken that airman is about to drop almost into his lap. Now listen,' he says more earnestly, 'there is only one road leading to his hide-out, Nicole, and it is very narrow – too narrow for this truck. So I am going to block it and pretend my engine has stalled. That will allow time for you to get up to the ruins of the old priory. You must stand in the arch at the east end and spread our arms across as though you are measuring the width of the opening. If he decides to speak to you he will come.'

'And you accuse me of playing games.'

'Just do as you are told,' he snaps. 'Did you think you just went up and knocked at the door? When they see who it is they may not even want to take the risk – I know I wouldn't.'

The truck swings into another lane where brambles and hawthorn branches scrape the sides and the wheels plough into the verges. This is the Bocage of Normandy, with its earth banks and its barricades of hedgerows with the intertwined roots of trees that defy tanks and make it ideal partisan country. It will take the Germans some time to locate the spot where the parachute landed even after they have assembled a search party. So, with luck, there should be time before they arrive to get the airman under cover. Whether the Colonel will wish to risk reprisals is another matter, and he might prefer to lie low until the commotion has died down before he ventures out of his hide-out, for in a short while the whole area is going to be crawling with German soldiers.

'Here we are,' Marcel announces as they grind down the last few metres of lane towards a small ford with a stream of muddy water crossing the road, and an even narrower lane leading off to the left. 'Hold it!' he shouts, and allows his truck to free-wheel down into the dip and career across the stream to come to rest with its bonnet stuck in the hedge. 'Away you go.' He pushes her out, pointing towards the lane. 'You must know the ruins. If no one comes in five minutes make your own way back, but don't come this way.'

'What about you?' she asks.

'I'll think of something. Don't stand there arguing. We haven't much time.' He turns his back on her and dives under the bonnet to fiddle with his engine as she scampers up the rutted track.

The ruins stand like broken teeth, black against the skyline, ignored by everybody except the most ardent of archaeologists, and overgrown with moss and lichen as they crumble into decay. A rabbit warren pockmarks the spiny turf, and every crevice in the masonry has its birds' nest. The doorway is easy to find for it is the only part of the old building of any substance. It has an arch of large, granite stones hanging on defiantly against wind and erosion. Once that goes the priory will be no more than man-made crags supporting the sky.

The air up here is heady with the scent and sounds of spring, and she suddenly realises that the bombing has stopped. Despite her sarcasm with Marcel, she feels a thrill of excitement at the prospect of meeting the notorious Colonel at last. He has become something of a legend amongst the defiant ones in the village. The stories of his daring raids are colourful and much exaggerated. Every incident of sabotage is attributed to him even though they often occur in different areas at the same time. She has often criticised what she considers to be his over-cautious method of doing things, and knows this is the main reason why he has never allowed her to come to his hide-out before. Now, at last, she will meet him and his heroic band of guerillas.

Meanwhile she swallows her annoyance at this ridiculous charade. Only men could think of such a childish method of contact, and she feels quite foolish standing there with her arms outstretched in the arch. The minutes go by and no one comes, if you discount the urchin who wanders up the sloping field with a disreputable mongrel at his heels. He is no more than twelve years old and his progress is erratic as he sends his dog on fruitless errands into the remote corners of the warren. How she is to judge when five minutes have passed without a watch is beyond her, but it must be getting close to that now. A hawk is hovering over the hedgerow, so she decides to wait for it to swoop as a signal for her to give up.

The harsh voice spins her round to face a group of men, and what she sees makes her heart sink. It looks as though every worthless scoundrel in the area is gathered there. She recognises the Flouquet twins who spend more time in prison than out, for they are the scourge of the village and one time beat up an old woman in her own home for a paltry sum of money, then wrecked her house for good measure. Now they stand with others of their kind festooned with bandoliers and brandishing automatic weapons.

'I ask again. What are you doing here?' The man who speaks is a cut above the rest in his dress and bearing. He wears a beret and a black, military-style tunic with no insignia. His face is swarthy with a heavy moustache and calculating eyes. The only weapon he has is a revolver which he carries in a side-holster.

'I am looking for the Colonel,' she says warily, conscious of the circle of smirking faces, and wishing she had not been so impetuous. She might have known that Marcel would associate with thugs like these.

'Why?' His face hardens. 'Answer, girl. I have no time for conversation. Your name is Nicole Martin – that much I do know, and you are a damn nuisance with your irresponsible ways. Someone is going to pay dearly for bringing you here if there is no good reason.'

She knows instinctively that he is the Colonel, and despite his theatrical appearance he has an air about him that demands respect, but when she looks round at the roguish lot that accompany him she is ready to give up in despair. Can these really be the romantic renegades that everyone raves about? 'Are you the Colonel?' she asks coldly.

His eyes flicker momentarily. He has no need to anwer. The look in his face tells that he enjoys his notoriety. 'That is as maybe. You have no choice now, whoever I am. We do not encourage visitors, Nicole. If you have come here on a fools' errand I will have to think hard about releasing you.'

'I did not know I was a prisoner.'

'Everyone is a prisoner who sets eyes on me, until I decide I can trust them. Come,' he adds impatiently, 'we know all about the airman. The Germans will be here soon to search for him and we are wasting time.'

The story spills out. The priest, Camille, Mathias, the radar and Marcel's part in all this. When she is done their blank stares reveal nothing. No one seems very impressed with anything she has told them. 'What are we supposed to do about all this?' the Colonel asks, glancing round at his men.

'I do not know,' she admits vaguely. 'All over France the Resistance is coming out into the open, and I have heard stories about you and your partisans. Surely we cannot leave the curé in their hands? I thought there might be a way of rescuing him. There is the soldier too. He knows the whole layout of their defences. Would not that knowledge be of value to you?'

He takes a couple of steps forward to stare straight into her eyes. 'Good God, girl! Do you know who we are?' He waves his hand at the gang. 'We are the FTP – French Irregulars and Partisans. We are organised by the Free French Forces of the

Interior – we are part of an army – a vast army. We do not become involved in petty local disputes. Not only do we fight to rid France of the Nazis, but we are going to bring a new communist system to this fascist state. Our orders come from the highest command and we will have a part to play in the invasion when it comes.'

He struts up and down in front of her, waving his arms about, full of himself, while his men look at him with a mixture of amusement and tolerance. A gang of freeloaders pandering to the whim of a self-opinionated revolutionary. 'What do we care about a deserter who deserves to die anyway? Or a priest who makes such a stupid spectacle of himself over the destruction of a church, when everyone knows churches will be destroyed by the dozen when the Allies invade and the fighting really starts. As for your airman – what would we do with him? He must take his chance and hide. And the radar – how do we know the deserter is even telling the truth?'

She flares up. 'So we do nothing about any of this? The SS parade through our village, incarcerate our priest and treat us like chattels. For four years we have had to live with these thugs. Telling us what to do, and even living in our homes. Dominating our lives, while those who should be leading the Resistance kowtow to them. I thought there were still some Frenchmen with blood in their veins.'

'Enough!' he raps, stopping her outburst mid-flow. 'You talk as stupidly as you act. The best thing you can do for us is to continue distributing your news-sheets, and tell Marcel anything you learn. After all,' he grins maliciously, 'your father is close to the German authorities. You must get to hear of many things that will be of use.' As though that answers all her problems he gives a curt order to his men: nods farewell, and they all go off, leaving her fuming amongst the ruins.

'Mademoiselle!' Now the scruffy lad is back with his dog.

'What do you want?' she demands ungraciously.

'I know where the airman is.' His face is intent as he kicks at a stone without looking at her, while his dog sits quietly at his side. 'I could take you to him.'

Without waiting for her to reply he leads the way out of the ruins and down a winding path that snakes through a craggy cleft until it opens out into a field with a small clump of trees making an island in the centre. They follow the dog who heads for the trees with his tail wagging excitedly.

Potter watches them from the shadows as they approach. He had been packing up his parachute in the field when the dog came bounding up. He had got on well with the boy thanks to his excellent French. The drop was easy enough after his engine began to act up, and he had been lucky to gain height before it packed up altogether. There was just time to order the others back to the carrier and release his canopy before the Corsair rolled into a spin. Now the boy is back with a girl and the skyline is clear, although the sound of an engine hangs in the air to remind him to keep well back in the shadows. The parachute is tucked well out of sight in a convenient hole created by the upturned root of a fallen tree, and he has checked through his flying suit for anything that might be of use to the enemy and buried that too. The few items of survival kit do not inspire a lot of confidence when you are alone in the middle of occupied country, but he stows them away carefully in his pockets.

The boy's eager face is full of pride as he brings her up to the hide-out. Potter winks at him then turns his attention to Nicole. 'Looks as though I am in your hands,' he says lamely. There is no encouragement in her expression. Nice-looking girl in a Romany way, but she scrutinises him as though he is a bit of a bloody nuisance.

'What am I supposed to do with you?' she asks blandly.

He is at a loss. 'Well, not you personally perhaps. The boy seemed to think you might help. Is there a local Resistance, or an escape route?'

The dog growls menacingly: the hair bristling on the back of his neck as he stares across the field. Almost at once they hear men's voices.

'Now what?' breathes Potter as they withdraw further into the copse.

'Stay here,' says the boy. 'I will tell them I saw you come down over there.' He points to a distant line of trees. The airman pats his shoulder as he moves out of the shadows with his dog, to wander across the stubbled turf in his aimless fashion towards the party of soldiers who emerge from a gate at the far end. They go down the hedgerows, looking into the drainage ditches, while half a dozen head directly for the trees. The boy is clever. He appears to ignore them: intent on urging his dog into rabbit holes. One of the leading soldiers shouts at him and he stops, looking at them, but making no move to go over. Someone raps an angry order at him in German. *'Venez! Venez!'* shouts another, beckoning with his rifle. The boy is not to be hurried. He shuffles across the field with his mongrel trailing suspiciously behind, its tail tucked well under its stern. They form a semi-circle round the boy, who stands looking up into their faces as though on trial.

'When did you last see your father?' whispers Potter.

'Sorry?'

'No matter,' he ignores her puzzled look and focuses on the tableau again.

The boy is acting his part well; looking stupid as they try to get through to him. He points vaguely towards a corner of the field, changes his mind while they curse his yokel mind, then points in a slightly different direction. Yes, he nods insistently. That is the direction for sure. Four go off at the trot, but two persist in coming towards the trees.

*

The Hauptmann is angry and protests violently to Müller, demanding that Mathias be turned over to the Wehrmacht, but the major refuses. 'We have no time for petty courts martial,' he snaps. 'We found the little rat hiding away, and it is plain he was helped by the priest. There is an element in this village that needs to be taught that they cannot disobey the orders of the military. Dissidents, communists, and the like, who, given the chance, will cause mischief everywhere. They seem to understand only draconian measures, Herr Hauptmann.

Therefore I think one sharp, painful lesson will convince them that we are the masters. Tomorrow morning we will take those who are locked in the school with the padre into the street and hang them from the lamp-posts with the deserter. We shall see then how many brave partisans will continue to disrupt our supply lines and stab us in the back.'

The sun climbs high into a cloudless sky, turning the street into an oven as word gets round the village about the executions, and Camille wanders into the centre of it all, walking like a zombie, oblivious to the cat-calls and snide remarks that follow her as she makes for her home. Only the strident wail of the air-raid siren saves her from further abuse as they hurry to take shelter and the guns open up just outside the village.

The Corsairs come in low over the coast, taking the garrison by surprise as they swoop down towards the village, strafing as they go. The 'stand to' klaxon blares out from the radar station, and the 37mm flak-guns burst into life as crews scramble to their posts. The aircraft soar up in steep climbs and disappear into the cloud, leaving the gunners squinting through their sights as their ears strive to follow the sound. Two Corsairs break cloud and howl down with their noses aimed straight at the sham radar aerial, releasing their bombs as they pull out of their dive. Immediately afterwards the other two appear, this time streaking in from the opposite direction in a shallow dive, using the bomb bursts as their marker, to deposit their five hundred pounders in the devastation caused by their companions. The attack is over in three minutes, and all that remains of the aerial is a twisted mass of scorched metal. The leader performs a classic victory roll as they circle round to form up for the flight home, while the Germans smirk with satisfaction at the way the ruse has worked; especially when they hear the tone of his engine change and begin to stutter. The eyes of occupiers and occupied watch fascinated as the little 'plane struggles to gain height before the blossoming parachute makes its slow descent. Cross-bearings show the spot where the pilot should land, and two lorries leave the barracks with search-parties.

The grim reality of war seems to have descended on the village like a curse. The old school is one of the more prominent buildings and when people pass by they try not to look at the SS guards on the door, or remember the faces of the condemned men inside. The small crowd at the wine bar crouch over their drinks in sombre mood with little to say. Etienne is isolated more than ever; without even the comfort of sitting quietly while the others discuss their trades and businesses, for today no one wishes to indulge in small-talk, and there are no words to describe their feelings about what will take place in the morning. At last it falls to one of the older men to break the awkward silence.

'Where is Nicole today, Etienne? I have not seen her since yesterday.'

The circle of eyes focuses on him. 'I do not know, Georges. I too have not seen her since she went off with the curé.'

'Are you not concerned?'

He looks up with sad eyes. 'Yes, I am concerned.'

The older man leans across to him. 'Things have changed, Etienne. This new German and his men no longer treat us like Frenchmen, and the other men who have been with us for so long – they are not the same. I think they are scared of the new soldiers.'

'Yes,' says another in a hushed voice. 'I feel it too. There is something new in the air. The Germans are nervous and, like a horse, when they get nervous they are unpredictable.' The talk dies as two of Müller's men patrol past with their rifles slung over their shoulders. They look in at the window at the circle of old men with expressionless faces, and the old men lower their heads and look away.

'I fought the Boche in the last war,' says Georges. 'They were not the same men as these.'

*

In the trees Nicole and Potter lie close to the fallen trunk listening to the two soldiers as they come towards their hiding place. There is nowhere to go. In a few seconds they must be discovered. The smell of fungus and rotting bark fills their nostrils as the gutteral voices get nearer. Suddenly there is a yell, followed by wild shouts, laughter and several rifle shots. Potter lifts his head warily to see the mongrel lolloping across the field in pursuit of a bunch of rabbits. The two troopers have left the copse to chase after them. Everyone joins in the game; even the NCOs are half-hearted in the way they admonish their men. It is a welcome relief to a boring search for an airman who isn't going to get far anyway. It is a Leutnant who brings order when he barks an order to one of his troops, who takes aim. The dog drops; turns two somersaults, and lies still with a bullet through his brain.

They return to their search. The trees are forgotten as they press on into the next meadow. The sounds die until only the scolding cornbuntings dominate the air with their scratching sound. Potter and Nicole slip away from the copse together. When they have gone the boy kneels by his dog and sobs.

She takes Potter to the cottage where he dresses in some of Le Clerq's clothing. 'You must stay here. There is food in the cupboard. Just try to keep out of sight,' she tells him. 'I am going to contact our local priest, he should know what to do. Now I must go, or I will be missed in the village.'

*

When she arrives in the village she can sense the sombre atmosphere. Even her mother is subdued, and the outburst she expected does not materialise. Apart from a mild rebuke they withdraw into themselves. Her father looks almost ill as he sits smoking in his chair, and their silence is unnerving. At last, unable to bear it any longer she asks, 'I would like to see the curé. Do you know where he is?'

They exchange looks and Etienne says, 'You don't know then?'

'Know what?'

His features seem to crumble. 'The curé is to be executed in the morning with several others. He is accused of aiding a deserter.'

'My God!' she exclaims. 'And these are the people you work for!'

His face reddens. 'How easy it is for you to accuse. You have been well clothed, well educated, and well fed all your life. Did you think it was easy? Do you not see the poverty round here? I did not make any agreements with the Germans – politicians did that. What was I supposed to do in your black and white world? Throw it all up? Let my family starve?' He calms down, staring into the grate with sad eyes. 'I am no hero, Nicole. I am a small man who finds it difficult even to survive. I am born to be dominated, and the only thing I can do is provide a good home for you and your mother. I can do no more.'

Her face softens, and she can see pity even in her mother's eyes. She turns to the window to look out at the sad houses with their blank doors and windows. 'I know,' she says quietly, 'but they are going to murder our priest.'

He looks at her beseechingly. 'If you know of anything I can do then tell me and I will gladly do it. Remember though, in this village we are alone if we go against the tide.'

'Are we?' Her mother's voice cuts in and they both look at her in surprise. It is seldom she speaks other than to nag him or complain. It is as though she feels that if she relents once it will undermine her status, but now her face is passive and her eyes full of hurt. 'I know it takes an earthquake to drag the locals out of their apathy, but perhaps this is the thing that will do it.'

'I don't know, mother. Most of them do not even go to church,' says Nicole.

'The priest is more than the church. He is part of the village. He marries us, baptises us, and buries us. When we see him hanged tomorrow, will not part of the village die with him?'

They have never heard her speak like this. Her forbidding facade has always been closed to sentiment, and when someone is needed who can be trusted not to show emotion she is the one they call on. She has laid out more villagers than anyone else, and shaken bereaved relatives back to reality with her blunt manner. Now she will not look at them, but her emotions show in her slumped shoulders and downcast head.

'If there was only something,' mutters Etienne sadly.

Nicole kneels in front of him and grips his soft hands. 'There is,' she stresses, squeezing his pulpy fingers. 'I have found the pilot of the aircraft that crashed. He is hiding in Father Le Clerq's cottage, and I am sure I can persuade Marcel to pick us up on the Caen road tomorrow. No one would think of looking for him in this house, father. We might even be able to get him away on an escape route.'

For a fleeting moment a cloud of fear shadows his face, but then he sets his mouth firm and looks up at his wife, who nods her agreement. 'All right, Nicole. Bring him here. If need be we can hide him until the Allies come.'

She stands up looking at them both, and seeing how ordinary they are. She would like to kiss her mother's craggy face but knows it would only embarrass her, and Etienne is choking back his anxiety with great difficulty. An emotional display might destroy his resolution. Curfew is almost here, so she must wait until tomorrow. The long hours of the night are going to seem interminable.

*

Müller's men are out early. The village installed new lighting just before the war, or rather they installed second-hand lighting that had been discarded in Caen, but the elegant streetlamps look ultra-modern amongst the old Normandy houses with their twin brackets and slender standards. They will make ideal gallows, and in their cold, efficient manner the SS troopers produce matching ladders; two to each post. One for the victim and one for the executioner, for it seems there is no shortage of proficient hangmen amongst Müller's men. By nine o'clock all is ready and two Panthers stationed at each end of the street ensure that it will remain traffic free while the executions are carried out.

The inhabitants who had determined to remain indoors

until it is all over do not reckon on Müller. His troopers hound them out of their homes until everyone, young and old alike, stands in the dusty street to witness the ritual. The SS line the kerbs, watching the crowd with their eyes shaded beneath their helmets, while the garrison troops are drawn up in two sections of three ranks with the Hauptmann in front, mounted on his horse. The major stands with a small knot of his own officers between two armoured half-tracks at the end of the street, ensuring that the scene is set before he nods at the waiting escort commander.

First come two Wehrmacht infantrymen with the distraught figure of Mathias propped between them. He wears a uniform now, but stripped of its buttons and insignia, and he has to be held upright as they march him to the first lamp-post, where they form up to wait for the other victims. The straggled line of men walk aimlessly out of the school, flanked by two files of SS troopers. Le Clerq leads them out, and as he walks he looks at the crowd of grim-faced villagers, picking out familiar faces and nodding every so often with a half-smile on his calm face. There are four others who walk as though in a daze, two dark-suited men who are almost strangers to the rest, for they had businesses in Caen and kept themselves to themselves in their big houses. It is said they are Freemasons. Then comes Jean, the blacksmith, who punched a German corporal for ill-using a mare and refused to apologise afterwards, and lastly there is Emil, the student, who was caught cutting a telephone wire and found with a revolver in his possession.

The silence hangs heavy in the street as they are made to climb the ladders and the nooses are placed over their heads. The only sound comes from Mathias who sobs uncontrollably, and has to be almost carried up the ladder. At Müller's signal their legs are kicked off the rungs and the lucky ones die with broken necks, while others kick and jerk as life is strangled out of them. Beneath the slumped body of Mathias a pool of urine spreads a dark patch in the dust, and it is all over.

The troops are marched away, and the villagers begin to filter back to their homes. Soon the whole street is deserted except for the patrols and one lone figure walking disconsolately towards the end lamp-past where Mathias swings with his eyes half-open. Camille looks up at him, white-faced and numb, until a couple of SS troopers turn up with a placard to hang round Mathias's neck. ' *'Raus, Fräulein! 'Raus!'* orders one, placing a hand on her arm and pushing her away. She moves a pace and stands staring at him with glazed eyes. He shrugs and says something to his mate in German that brings a chuckle, but they ignore her while one climbs the ladder with his notice.

They are interrupted by the sergeant from the party who found Mathias at the cottage. The man with the notice makes no move to climb down and the sergeant yells at him again. Several other soldiers are taking notice now, and the SS men are looking for one of their NCOs to tell this Wehrmacht intruder to go about his own business, but a couple of the sergeant's men arrive and the SS think better of it and back down. The sergeant himself goes up the ladder to lower the body into the arms of his men, then he climbs down again and takes Camille by the elbow to lead her several metres away. She is pale, dry-eyed and dazed, and he needs to push her gently on her way so that she walks automatically towards her home. He turns back to his men.

'Get Hans with his horse and cart. We will take this one back to barracks.'

'What of the others?' asks a trooper.

'They are not our concern.'

'Sergeant!' Müller's face is at the bakery window. 'What are you doing?'

'Taking my man back to his barracks, Herr Major,' he answers, snapping his heels together.

Müller crams his cap hard on his head and comes striding out into the street, red-faced. 'By whose orders?'

'No orders, sir.' He stares stolidly ahead.

'Put him back where he belongs. He will remain there as a warning to others for as long as it suits me.' When the sergeant hesitates he threatens. 'Do it, sergeant, or I will put you up there in his place for disobeying an order.'

'Herr Major!' The level voice of the Hauptmann intervenes. 'Will you leave our dirty washing out for all to see?'

'I say put him back. I order you to put him back, Hauptmann.'

The iron-shod wheels of the cart grate on the hard surface as it is brought up to the scene. Men of both sides are attracted to what is going on as the two officers shape up to each other. There is a great deal at stake here, for the local garrison have been forced to suffer the arrogance of the SS, because the major outranks their commander, for long enough and now they see him facing up to Müller, they group together. For a moment in the quiet street, with the dead eyes of the hanging corpses watching over them the two factions of the Third Reich defy each other.

'Herr Major,' the Hauptmann says quietly. 'Even in Germany we do not hang a man twice for being a coward.'

Müller has difficulty containing himself, but the episode has gone far enough. 'To continue this would be bad for discipline and morale, Herr Hauptmann. Take your deserter away from my sight. A full report will be made regarding your attitude. The Führer asks for total dedication, especially of his officers. Without it, how can we expect to win?'

Mathias's body is stretched out on the bare boards and the cart rumbles off. The other corpses are left to hang until mid-afternoon, when SS men cut them down. This time the Hauptmann does not interfere, and they are taken away to be thrown into a pit. It is while they are being loaded onto a truck that Marcel drives his lorry into the village and stops for a moment at Etienne's house. While all eyes are focused on the macabre scene at the end of the street no one notices Potter walk swiftly into the open door. The first heavy drops of an approaching downpour splatter in the dust, and in a few moments the drains are gurgling as the street is washed clean.

Five

Cyclops receives orders to proceed south-west and rendezvous with a support group of bird-class sloops to provide anti-submarine patrols ahead of a convoy heading up-channel. Once the convoy is past the Eddystone Light she is to leave them and proceed to Falmouth to take on fuel and supplies, then carry out repairs in time to take part in the forthcoming invasion. The captain is satisfied that their first serious mission was successful. Photographs show a bridge destroyed and several aircraft caught on the deck when they raided the airfield. During the whole show the Luftwaffe presented no threat at all so they were able to carry out low level attacks on military convoys to their hearts' content, and the radar station is a complete write-off. The loss of one aircraft through engine failure was the only casualty. Therefore the profit and loss accounts show a healthy balance in the carrier's favour. There was a general sigh of relief when the big blunt bows swung away from the French coast, however, and they were able to steam out into the relative safety of the broad Atlantic once more, for there were misgivings about taking her so close into the shore, within easy range of enemy airfields.

'D'you hear there! D'you hear there! The ship will go to "dawn action stations" in fifteen minutes' time.' That warning will stop the stampede of a real alert when the bugle sounds, and some men will already be on their way so they can take over their positions, test communications and get settled before the rush starts. Right forward in the narrow passageway of the cell block the marine sentry phones to ask if his prisoner must be released to go to his action station.

'No,' he is told. 'It is only routine and "stand down" will be sounded very shortly, once the first air patrol has been flown off,' and that response is typical of the slap-happy attitude that has developed towards the dawn and dusk action stations.

The commander is anxious to get outstanding work carried out, and impatient to get back to 'defence stations' so that he can get the off-duty seamen turned-to for an hour or so. He runs a taut ship and accepts no excuses when his eagle eyes latch onto a frayed rope or a patch of rust, so it has become accepted practice to excuse a man from his action station to carry out pressing jobs, on the theory that providing only one or two out of a ship's company of over a thousand are used, it will not affect the whole picture. When the ADR crew arrive they are met by a petty officer at the door who tells them to remain in the passage because a general tidy-up is taking place inside where a fastidious ADO is determined to clear away the stagnant remains of a long night.

On the flight deck the first patrol is preparing to take-off. Four Corsairs shudder to the vibrations of their engines as *Cyclops* turns up-wind. They launch into a grey sky and form up over a pewter sea with a clean horizon. Once they are clear the carrier rolls easily as she leaves the eye of the wind and falls into station with her destroyers. On her bridge men huddle in to their duffelcoats against the keen Atlantic breeze and their helmets are placed into convenient nooks close by in case they are required. The atmosphere is relaxed and everyone waits for the captain's decision to 'stand down'.

The port watch is due to take over at eight o'clock and the men they relieve will have an hour or so for breakfast before turning-to for the fore-noon. They know the sooner the chores are done the more break they will get before taking over again at twelve-thirty. In a two watch system, interrupted with 'stand-to' periods, every chance is taken to skive off for a smoke. Even though a few hard-nosed NCOs like PO Envoldsen make themselves unpopular by roaming about the ship chasing men out of the heads or the messdecks and are roundly cursed for their raucous voices and uncompromising discipline.

In his radar cabin Mort trains his scanner round meticulously. He has carefully tuned and calibrated his set to perfection, and cut off from the rest of the ship he concentrates on the display, watching the dancing peaks for every fluctuation. To him this is far superior to staring into the bland dials of the more sophisticated PPIs with their bars of light automatically sweeping round, painting contacts. His set must be operated with single-minded purpose, and a man's mind tuned in for the least suspicion of a contact. It is inevitable that such conscientiousness will one day be rewarded, and now, while those in the ADR are diverted for vital seconds while they make way for someone to dust round and clear away ash-trays, Mort finds his contact.

'Radar – Plot!' he calls into his mouthpiece and the man with the chinagraph pencil standing behind the big perspex screen with its spiderweb grid makes his mark on the screen with the time alongside.

'Bogey – zero eight five – seventy thousand yards,' the voice warns the bridge.

'Where did that come from?' asks the Air Direction Officer.

'The 79b, sir.'

'Anything on the 281?'

'No, sir. But we are getting interference from that area.'

The plotter makes a second mark and joins the two together with an arrow. 'Still nothing on the 281?' They are leaning forward in their seats. An aircraft travelling at two hundred miles an hour takes little more than ten minutes to cover the thirty-five miles from that reported position to the carrier.

'Vector zero nine zero – angels one zero.' The orders go out to the patrolling Corsairs who climb and bank unto their new heading.

'Port twenty,' replies Wally down in the wheelhouse as he runs the spokes through his hands to bring the bows back into the wind. On the flight-deck the clang-clang-clang of the warning bell sounds as the after lift is raised with a Corsair squatting with its wings folded.

'The 281 has contact, sir. Several aircraft.' Petty Officer Knight reports possible multi-engined types amongst them. Knight is noted for his ability to study the white arc of an echo and detect the oscillations caused by propeller blades to determine whether an aircraft is multi-engined or not. Most of his colleagues are sceptical, but Knight has proved himself right too many times to be ignored.

The gut-knotting scream of the bugle blares through the ship's tannoy. 'Bomber overhead! Bomber overhead! Bomber overhead!' it shrieks, sending feet rattling up ladders and into passages. The alarm is for real now, and men are anxious to be at their stations before the action starts.

'Pilots, man your aircraft!' shouts the flight deck tannoy, and men run out in flying suits as the wind comes fore and aft.

Mort's steady reports bring the chinagraph pencil track nearer and nearer to the centre of the web. 'Stand to aircraft port – bearing zero eight five!' The muzzles of the bofors and pom-poms nose the air as they train onto the bearing.

'Tally ho!' repeats the radioman in the ADR as he gets the first sighting from the group leader of the four Corsairs. 'Bogeys in sight, sir,' he translates as he listens to the taut voices in his earphones. 'Twenty plus aircraft – Heinkel 111s and Junkers 88s, fitted with Lichtenstein antennae. Heading straight for *Cyclops*.'

'That's interception radar, sir,' explains Commander Air to the captain. 'They use it in conjunction with the big Würzburgs set up on shore. It's bringing them straight to us.'

'That station we destroyed was supposed to be the only operational one in this area according to the boffins,' protests the captain.

'Well, they must have another, and they must be homing in on our aircraft, because we are below their horizon. Stand by – here they come,' he adds as one of the destroyers opens up with her four point sevens.

A telephone whines. 'The after lift is jammed, sir,' calls a pale-faced midshipman. 'They cannot get it to move up or down, and there's a Corsair on it.'

The lookouts are reporting aircraft now. Heinkels low down on the horizon, and skeins of Junkers high up, flying sedately through the clouds in rigid formation. The sky fills with black and brown bursts of anti-aircraft shells from the heavy guns of the destroyers, and now *Cyclops* adds her percussion to the symphony when her light guns begin their chorus.

'The Corsairs are under attack by Focke Wulf 190s, sir,' announces the radioman in a steady voice. 'They came out of the cloud.'

The ADO looks sick. 'Christ! We should have known!' he gasps.

On the bridge the message comes through like the voice of doom. 'Port thirty!' orders the captain abruptly as the first Heinkel roars in with its belly almost on the water. Tracer streams out in converging arcs, but it holds its course through a curtain of gunfire, and those with binoculars see the torpedo bounce twice before it settles on track for the ship. The carrier is slow to respond and her ponderous weight is reluctant to come round. To men on her deck it is as though she remains still while the whole kaleidoscope of the battle rotates round them.

Two more aircraft grow out of the grey dawn, wavering slightly as they make their approach into the barrage, but they seem immune to the torrent of fire until a plume of black smoke suddenly pours from an engine and a wounded Heinkel drops its torpedo and strives to gain height. To those on number four bofors, it seems to fill the sky before it explodes amongst them. The mass of wreckage spilling over the flight-deck incinerates the pilot of a stranded Corsair as he struggles to release his harness, and exploding petrol-tanks hurl their contents into the open lift and engulf the aircraft still sitting with its wings folded.

In his cell Malloy bangs frantically on the door, yelling at the marine sentry as he tries to summon help from a dead telephone. 'Eh! Get me aht of 'ere, fer Christ's sake! Come on, yer stupid bootneck bastard!'

The marine is in a nightmare of indecision. The last order he received was to stay on sentry duty and keep his prisoner locked up. Now the whole scene is changed and there is no one to tell him what to do. There is a telephone in the next compartment, but to reach it he must go through a 'Y' door, and it is against regulations to open X and Y openings at action stations.

'Oi!' bellows the AB. 'Read yer fuckin' instructions, can't yer? They tells yer ter let prisoners get to their action stations. Come on, yer gormless sod! Let me aht!'

The sentry hesitates for a second or so then opens the cell door. Malloy pushes past him with an oath and starts knocking the clips off. Once the door is open he plunges through into the next compartment, leaving the marines to shut it behind them. Just before he manages to get the first clip on the torpedo hits the bow and the explosion rips a huge hole in the ship's side, and her anchor cables roar out of their lockers into the empty depths of the ocean as water begins to pour in. Malloy is thrown off his feet, but recovers quickly to run on blind through the messdecks, leaving doors open as he goes. Marine sentries are posted on access doors and hatches to stop men from running below. So when Malloy comes hurtling up from the bowels of the ship he takes one by surprise as he rushes out onto the starboard maindeck.

On this side of the ship everything seems to be in order, except for a heavy pall of smoke pouring out across the sea from somewhere aft of the 'island'. Instinct tells him that it is all happening on the port side. The guns are chattering away and he can hear the sounds of aircraft. He jumps as the bofors on the sponson above bursts into life and a shadow swoops with black crosses on each wing to lift clear in a long, climbing turn.

The Junkers have the spotlight now as they come in steadily in a loose formation, their target half obliterated by smoke, tinged with yellow flame as it pours from the lift. They concentrate on the carrier, making their runs from three sides to split the barrage. *Cyclops* puts her helm over again, carving a wide furrow as she tries to spoil the aim of the bombers. Her head is down as the sea gushes in through the open bulkhead door to fill the next compartment, and her propellers lift clear as she begins to list.

With their bomb-bays gaping the Junkers come in. The yawning gap of the open lift seems to attract the first bomb when it leaves the black-bellied aircraft to arc down into the inferno. It bounces off the armour-plating and careers into the hangar before exploding in the midst of the stacked aircraft. A huge ball of fire rolls down the length of the hangar deck, engulfing men and machines as it goes. It roasts flesh, melts cables, sets off belts of ammuntion and in a supreme act of triumph explodes two five hundred pound bombs to blow out the side of the ship.

Another bomb pierces the thin plate of the Admiral's bridge and erupts in a billowing volcanic burst of smoke and flame. No longer under command *Cyclops* slumps over with a bow-down angle and a heavy list as a blast of super-heated steam roars from her safety valve like the dying gasp of a crippled monster. No one doubts any more that she is finished, and the order to abandon ship is relayed by word of mouth through her passages and compartments. As though to put a final seal on her fate a boiler bursts and her heart stops beating.

One of the destroyers circles towards the carrier as men begin to leap overboard. She moves in to place her bow under the stern, with her guns still firing at the diving aircraft, and through the mess a lone Corsair howls out of the sky with two Focke Wulf 190s on its tail. It pulls out of a steep dive to follow a Junkers as it finishes its bombing run. The big bomber roars away at masthead height with the little Corsair chasing after it and the two fighters swoop like hawks onto a wounded sparrow. The Corsair does a half-roll to plunge into the sea with the blades of its propeller taking it deep into the cold body of the Atlantic.

The angle of the flight-deck sends men sliding through burning fuel over the edge of the safety nets into the sea, where they struggle in a mass of debris to get clear of the massive bulk of the carrier. The destroyer is right up to her now, running

her bull-ring into the carrier's flank while her crew urge
Cyclops' men to jump. A violent explosion splits the port side
amidships, spewing out steam and smoke.

Mort hears awesome crashings as the tower of superstructure above him caves in. He can feel the heat as the flames
envelop the bridges and eat their way down through the
various chartrooms and offices filled with vital, combustible
equipment. No one is replying to his voice on the intercom,
and already he can smell the acrid tang of burning rubber as
cables begin to ignite. He thrusts open the door against the list
of the ship, heaves his body out into the passage and struggles
up the slope until he reaches the flight deck. The sight that
greets him is one of utter chaos. It seems the whole after end of
the carrier is ablaze, and every man is intent on saving his own
skin as they bustle about like ants. He has to crawl on hands
and knees to reach the port safety nets, where the vast cliffside
of scorching metal slants down to the sea. Her bilges are
showing, crusted with barnacles and seaweed, and men rip
their flesh on the jagged edges as they slide down.

He looks about him desperately for some means of lowering
himself, suddenly aware that the guns have ceased firing and
there is only the roar of the flames, screaming men and the
detonations of internal explosions. He turns aft in time to see
an apparition shrouded in flames climb out of the lift to rise
up on its feet and stagger to the low side of the ship. It makes
no sound as it hurls itself into the turbulent water. Shocked
and stunned he sees other men appearing from everywhere,
and when he looks towards the stern he can see the bridge and
mast of the destroyer waiting to take them to safety.

There is no way he can reach it from the flight-deck, so he
drops down into a sponson and through the passage that runs
behind. By some miracle it is still intact, although the paint is
blistering on the inboard side with the intense heat of the
raging fires just beyond. He scrambles aft onto the quarterdeck
as the carrier lifts its stern to an even more incredible angle. He
sees men grouped together at the farthest end, taking turns to
drop down onto the destroyer's fo'c'sle.

There is no panic or fighting for places and he can recognise Petty Officer Envoldsen bullying them into line to take their turn on the ropes that have been rigged over the guardrails, while injured men are being lowered with the aid of a pulley. In the midst of all the mess Mort has to grin: Trust that old bastard to get things organised. It is a desperate situation, however, for the destroyer is having its work cut out to keep position, and her seamen are dragging huge fenders about to protect their ship as she rolls against the carrier.

Mort takes his place alongside the PO who keeps up a monologue of threats and abuse as they guide the men over. 'If yer don't move yerself, Turner,' he yells at some hesitant OD, 'I'll 'ave yer doublin' wiv a rifle over yer 'ead until yer arms drop off.' Between them they feed the survivors over the side until there is no one left but themselves.

'Come on,' shouts the PO. 'No sense in 'anging' abaht.'

'Hang on,' protests Mort. 'There's blokes on the flight deck. They should be able to get through the starboard passage easy enough if someone leads them down to it. I'll go up and give them a hand.'

Envoldsen nods. 'Okay. I'll stay 'ere and make sure the destroyer don't shove orf wivaht us.'

The leading hand races forward, using handholds on the outboard bulkhead to keep well clear of the inboard side where the blistering heat is enough to scorch a man's body. He is amazed at the number of men crowded on the rim of the flight deck. Masses of them, all lined up waiting for a chance to get clear of their sinking ship. There are two officers amongst them who take charge with the aid of several NCOs and begin shepherding the men to safety.

*

Wordsley recovers slowly after being knocked unconscious when the bomber devastated the mounting and killed his colleagues. He had been in the passage behind the sponson when the aircraft hit, helping to pass boxes of ammunition up from a chain gang formed to replace the automatic hoist that was put out of action. Dazed he looks about at the smoking ruins, trying to re-establish himself. There are shouts from above his head, and the rumble of internal explosions below, and his first reaction is to climb up onto the flight-deck. But the charred, skeletal remains of the Heinkel prevent that. When he moves the slope of the deck sends him careering towards the inboard bulkhead that feels hot to his touch. He fights down a growing panic as he realises how badly wounded the carrier must be to be set at this angle. He must get up top; that's the first thing. Just below is the main-deck with its passageway fore and aft the whole length of the ship. Once there, he should be able to find his way. The ladder leads down to a cross-passage that runs athwartships for its entire width, and the door leading to it is just off the sponson. He is about to open it when the heated surface makes him pause.

'Christ!'

He spins round, staring horrified at the tangled mass that blocks the sponson.

'I'm trapped!' he croaks, gulping down the fear and fighting to keep his thoughts in order.

The only way out is through that door, yet there is no way of knowing what lies beyond it. The whole passage could be a raging inferno, just waiting for the inrush of air to trigger an explosion. Gingerly he tests the steel with cautious fingers. Forward of the door the bulkhead is almost too hot to bear, but the door itself and the after bulkhead are cooler. There are two clips. He knocks them off easily, holding the door shut with his weight while he takes another deep breath, bolstering his courage before carefully easing it open, using it as a shield against whatever lies beyond.

Nothing! There is no smoke or smell. He peers round into the dark corridor. It is like looking down a pit-shaft. The ventilation trunking and the mass of cables and support girders disappear into the gloom only a few yards in, and the passage is invisible at the far end. The air is stagnant and hot, but not unbearably so. The hatch he seeks is only a couple of yards inside and it has no lid. Hopefully he edges into it and peers down into a scene of devastation. A gaping hole opens like a crater to the sea, for this is where their own five hundred pound bombs ruptured her side.

Now what? he asks himself. It is pointless to go back. There is another hatch on the starboard side, but the slope of the deck tells him that the passage there is probably below the surface. He stares into the black void at the far end. There is no sponson on that side, for that is where the 'island' is situated. The 'island'! Of course!

There are a number of doors with ladders leading up into the complex structure. He has to lean back against the slope as he edges cautiously down its length. If anything the passage cools as he descends towards the other end, but the shadows grow deeper as he goes into the black abyss where all light is excluded and all sound magnified.

He is using the after bulkhead as a support, testing each move with a tentative foot. He feels utterly alone in this huge ship with its ominous noises. He can no longer hear the shouting, and the only human sound is his own strangled breathing. There can be no doubt that the ship is sinking. Even now he could be below the water-line, with only the flimsy upperdeck doors between him and the ocean. Thankfully he reaches the end. Now he must think. Try to recall the layout of this unfamiliar area. On the starboard side there are several doors leading into the base of the 'island' itself, but before he reaches them there is an open hatch leading down to the main-deck where the wheelhouse is situated. Must avoid that as he goes aft.

A long, drawn-out groan freezes him. 'Who's that?' he croaks through a tight throat. The only reply is another groan. An overwhelming surge of joy comes as he realises he is not alone. Even if whoever is making that sound is injured it is another human being in this metallic hell.

'I'm coming!' he calls. 'Hold on. I'm coming!'

He works his way through the pitch black until he can hear breathing. His shuffling foot finds something soft and another groan comes from below. He bends and feels about until he locates an arm and a hand.

'You okay, mate?' he asks stupidly.

His probing tells him the arm is hooked over the rim of the hatch, while the remainder of the body is on the ladder below. There is a faint light down there. Not enough to filter into the passage, but sufficient to recognise Wally's bulk and the way he is clinging to the ladder. There doesn't seem to be a mark on him, and certainly no blood anywhere.

'Where does it hurt, Wally?' asks the OD, but the only answer is yet another groan. He reaches under the armpits and hauls up gently, tensing for the scream of agony he feels sure must come. Nothing – just the laboured breathing, punctuated by a series of groans. He tries harder, but the torso is too heavy and he cannot budge him one inch. A grinding sound tightens his inside as the ship moves beneath him. What the hell can he do? That vague light from below doesn't penetrate the passage and he is in solid blackness with no one to turn to for help. He agonises for a moment until a loud creak echoes through the hull. He must go or she will take him down with her. There's nothing he can do for Wally now, and it is no good both of them dying down here in the darkness. He is almost sobbing when he straightens up.

'Up top!' The voice drags him down to the hatch again to peer down into the gloom, trying to recognise who is shouting. 'Is there anyone there?' It's Malloy's voice, tinged with anxiety. Of all men, it has to be him. 'Help me get this body aht of the way, whoever you are.'

'It isn't a body. It's Wally; and he's alive. Give us a hand up with him.' There is no reply, but he can hear feet on the iron rungs and Wally's torso shifts a little. He takes another grip on the armpits and between them they move the helmsman inch by inch until he is stretched out on the deck; wedged in the angle where it meets the outboard bulkhead.

'Come on,' says Malloy. 'We ain't got much time. Where's the door, for Christ's sake!'

'We'll have to be careful with him, Malloy. He must be injured bad.'

'You stupid sod! You don't think we're gonna try to drag that bloody great lump with us, do yer? 'E's ad it anyway. If we don't get crackin' nah, we'll go dahn wiv 'er.'

'We're not going to go off without him,' protests Wordsley.

'You can do what the fuckin' 'ell yer like, mate. Me! I'm gettin' aht of 'ere before the whole bloody lot goes dahn.'

Wordsley stands up to grope his way along until he finds Malloy. He might be timorous when bullied by superiors, but Malloy doesn't scare him any more. He grabs a fistful of the AB's clothing and wrenches him round so that he can yell straight into his face. 'We ain't gonna leave Wally down here, mate. Like it or not, you're gonna help me to get him up top out of it.'

For a moment Malloy struggles to break free. 'Bah!' he spits out finally. ' 'Ow many sugar daddies 'ave yer got? Trust me ter get mixed up wiv a wet-nosed sprog. Come on then. Stop pissin' abaht.'

Together they manhandle Wally along the passage until they reach a door. When they release the clips and pull it open blessed light shines through. True the air is full of sulphurous smoke, but now, at last, they can see. Step by step they ease their burden up the steel ladder into the small passage that runs by Mort's radar office, and they can see bright daylight streaming through the open door leading out onto the flight deck.

*

Mort is urging the last few remaining men down into the main passage when Envoldsen suddenly appears alongside him. 'Right lad. It's time ter leave. I knew I'd find yer still 'angin' abaht up 'ere, yer silly sod. It's everyone for 'imself now, and that bloody destroyer ain't gonna be there much longer, 'cause the stern is comin' down on top of 'er. Come on, let's get the 'ell out of it while we still can.'

The leading hand needs no second bidding. He can see the carrier settling rapidly, and already the leading edge of the flight deck is dipping below the surface as one compartment after another fills. He goes to scramble over the side when Envoldsen shouts. 'Heh! What the 'ell's that?'

Mort follows his outstretched arm to see a small group of struggling men emerge from the door leading into the 'island'. Without further ado they run across the deck to where the two men are dragging Wally out into the smoky sunshine.

'What's wrong with 'im?' asks the PO.

'Dunno,' replies Wordsley. 'He looks bad. He's bin unconscious since we found him halfway up a ladder.'

Mort bends down and peers into the fat man's face and winces. 'He's as pissed as a newt,' he says laconically. 'That's what's wrong with him. I can smell the bubbly on his breath.'

'Bloody hell!' protests Malloy. 'Yer means ter tell me I've bin riskin' me neck fer a piss-artist?'

'Never mind that now,' snarls Envoldsen. 'Let's get 'im across and down to the destroyer.'

Cyclops has one more trick up her sleeve, however. Avgas escaping from a ruptured tank spews out through empty water jackets that should have kept it safely bottled. Vapour fills the area of flats and passages, building a lethal mixture that needs only a small spark to ignite, and there is no shortage of such sparks in *Cyclops* today.

The explosion when it comes supersedes all else. It tears out the guts of the carrier, while expanding forces twist and buckle metal as though it is tinsel. The whole fore-end that up to now has remained relatively undamaged erupts with a violence that shatters the air. Crews on the destroyers look up horrified as a towering mass of flame and smoke envelops the ship. It is as though the very steel is burning. There seems no part of her that is not aflame. Ammunition in ready-use lockers, and on the guns begins to explode. In her death throes she is a raging beast, maddened by the wounds she has sustained, spitting fire and roaring in agony. Even the sea turns molten as oil spews out in a spreading mass of flame. The destroyer's screws churn frantically to pull her clear of the inferno. Men still cling to the ropes and guardrails, yelling at her as she goes astern to leave them stranded. Some are thrown into the sea to struggle in a nightmarish quagmire of choking oil while the huge propellers and rudder loom over them.

The little group near the 'island' turn with one accord and drag Wally into the sheltered side of the crane-deck. Here the flight deck is almost at sea level and eight Carley rafts are secured along the out-board side of the 'island'. Mort and Envoldsen clamber up to reach the release gear of the nearest raft and manage to free it so that it floats out amongst a spreading flotsam. Mort swims to it and hauls his body unto the framework. *Cyclops* is finished now as a crescendo of violent explosions tears her asunder and blasts her open to the sea. A line lashes his shoulders and he reaches blindly for it, hauling it in hand over hand as the huge shape of the 'island' leans out over him. They struggle together to heave Wally's inert bulk on board, then they are shoving off while Mort uses his knife to cut free the lashings on the paddles. They paddle desperately away from her as she seems to be on the point of taking her last roll, and her shadow reaches out to them as they drift clear.

A destroyer is whooping excitedly on her siren to draw attention to a signal hoisted at her yard as she responds to a contact on her asdics. Somewhere beneath the surface the black shapes of U-boats attracted like hyenas to the bloated corpse of the sinking carrier close in. There is no room for sentiment now. A static ship is a dead ship when submarines are lining up with torpedoes, so the vague chance of a few swimmers remaining alive in the cauldron of burning oil and garbage is too remote to warrant risking a ship. As though to emphasize this the black-ened carcass slumps her bow right under and the propellers lift high in the air as she prepares for her last dive. HMS *Cyclops*, a luckless carrier, has not had time to flex her muscles, and the Luftwaffe has one final moment of triumph before it becomes an impotent, second-rate force in the new struggle for Europe. The destroyers chase shadows, no longer sure if there are submarines there, but eager to get away from the area where the disgorged remains of the big ship scar the ocean. They form up in line astern with their clean white wakes spreading while the angry eyes of the men on the raft stare after them.

Now the world seems an empty place with the cold swell of the Atlantic rocking their tiny refuge. A search of the waterproof containers produces emergency rations of food, water and flares. The low silhouettes of the departing destroyers are too far away to notice and soon drop over the horizon, but they tell themselves that this is a busy part of the ocean, so they are certain to be picked up before long.

The sinister shape of the U-boat broaches less than fifty yards away with men pouring over the rim of her bridge almost before she has settled to an even keel. Black exhaust drifts across the surface from her stern as her diesels idle while she wallows amongst the wreckage. She makes no move to close on the raft, but the wind is drifting them down towards her. Cold, hostile eyes peer at each other as she gets nearer, and a heaving-line snakes out to fall across them. Wally's eyes open to look about him with a vague look of incomprehension. The sleek bow of the submarine cuts into the open sky above his head and he can feel cold water slopping round his ample rump.

'Oh God,' he groans, holding his throbbing head. 'That's all I need – fucking DTs.'

'Oh you've come to, 'ave yer?' growls Envoldsen without sympathy. 'Come on, get up. The opposition's arrived. Mustn't let 'em see what we're really like.'

The raft is bumping alongside the U-boat now, and hands reach down to help them climb the slippery side of the ballast tanks onto her casing. They are urged along towards the conning tower with sharp commands and prods. Wally staggers behind with his head held in his hands as he tries to sort something sensible out of this crazy situation. He has always taken the bottle on watch with him, filled with neat rum, so that an occasional nip could help him through long, boring periods on the wheel. When the 'abandon ship' order came, and it seemed the 'island' was about to crash in on him he had ordered the two telegraphsmen to try and save themselves before he shut the wheelhouse door. The carrier was dying and he could hear the mad scramble going on outside. With his bulk he stood no chance, so he uncorked his bottle and drank it down in long, satisfying gulps, and everything had dissolved into a whirlpool of distorted hallucination.

The Germans are impatient as they chase the survivors along, eager to get their boat down out of the limelight. As soon as they reach the bridge they are pushed through the conning tower hatch and hustled forward to the fore-ends where they are made to sit on stools each side of a central table that runs fore and aft down the length of what looks like a sewer. They hear a series of orders and the submarine seems to heave a deep sigh before the thunder of her diesels stops and all goes quiet. In a few moments they hear the gurgle of water above their heads and realise they are beneath the surface. It all seems cosy and warm, despite the stench and the only sound is the muted whine of the electric motors, the occasional slither of oily hydraulics, and the mutter of men's voices.

'What do you reckon about this then?' asks Mort. 'It ain't like this lot to pick up survivors.'

'Maybe her skipper's a charitable bloke,' muses Envoldsen without conviction.

They sit uneasily while the submarine crew come and go without any attempt at communication. Eventually an officer wearing a white, battered cap arrives and studies them for a moment before speaking in perfect English.

'We have no more spare clothing I regret, but my men will make you as comfortable as possible. We do not usually pick up survivors and you will be asking yourselves why we have taken you on board.'

He studies each of their faces in turn. His face is gaunt and bearded with tired, intelligent eyes. Like his crew he is part of the boat, with her sweat ingrained in his sallow skin, and there is an air about them all that says they are professionals.

'You are lucky. Tomorrow we should reach port, and you will be taken ashore. If you wish your luck to continue you will be co-operative. Remember, we already know that you are part of the preparations for an invasion. Nothing you can say to us will add to what we already know. You are only pawns in a bigger game, but life will be much easier for you if you answer questions truthfully. In the meantime, if you have anything to tell me, you have only to ask the sentry. I will see you all at once, or individually. Until then, rest well and think hard.' He turns to go, and his place is taken by a seaman with a sub-machine gun.

'There's your answer, mate,' states Envoldsen after a while. 'They think we know where the invasion is gonna take place.'

'Bloody hell!' scoffs Mort. 'What do they think we are, poxy admirals?'

'Nevertheless, don't give more than yer 'ave ter away. Yer name, rank and serial number is all they're entitled to. They ain't picked us up fer sod-all.' He looks up at the sentry. 'Can I 'ave a drink of water, mate?' The features remain blank. It doesn't mean a lot though, for the man probably wouldn't let on if he could speak English anyway, and it would make sense to have someone handy who could understand what they are saying.

The boat is preparing for her approach to Cherbourg. Her commander is well aware of the hazards they face, and the signal that ordered him to surface and pick up the survivors could only originate from a military mind with no conception of the perils involved. The Allies have sophisticated radar now, and a U-boat has only to poke her bridge above the water to bring the hounds of hell down on her. The worst part of any patrol is getting in and out of base, and his crew are war weary with their nerves stretched. They know full well how important it is to make their approach in secret, and wallowing exposed while they pick up a few wretched survivors is not their favourite pastime. It is enough that they are asked to carry out patrol after patrol with no future. Their families are bombed, their homes devastated. All the time the odds mount up against them. Not one of the Britishers is above the rank of petty officer, so it is extremely unlikely that they have any intelligence of real value.

The reason, could he but know it, stems from the attack on

the radar station. It is quite obvious that the type of aircraft used comes from an aircraft carrier, and the British do not risk capital ships without good cause. With the ominous threat of invasion looming, the High Command is as anxious to find out why, and for once the three services act in unison for a combined operation to sink *Cyclops* and, if possible, draw off her escort and pick up a survivor or two. The whole exercise is amazingly successful, except that the survivors are small fry. Nevertheless, experts can glean a surprising amount of information from the most innocuous remarks made by men when they are coaxed into talking of their home, their ship and the ports they come from.

Meanwhile the U-boat steals through the night while her crew rotate their watches. They are tense, hardly daring to breathe as the French coast draws nearer. The prisoners remain silent, sensing the strain. Some of the pale faces about them are old beyond their years, with haunted eyes and tight mouths. There is a fair amount of quiet banter between them, but the laughter is subdued and forced, as though it is merely to boost their morale. Mort watches thoughtfully. This is something he never reckoned on. These blokes clamped down in their metal cylinder for weeks on end with only the occasional glimpse of daylight and the ever-present threat of attack must live every second of every hour on their nerves. They must bear it without knowing what goes on up top half the time, for only one man ever sees the whole picture. The wonder is that Germany can still find such men, when even the most moronic must know that there is no future for them.

This time Lady Luck smiles on them. Mainly because the Allies are concentrating on the Biscay bases, and she slips through the cordon of patrolling ships to pick up her escort right on schedule. By dawn she has negotiated the mine-fields and comes under the protection of the big guns of Cherbourg. Inside the breakwater her casing party break out their ropes and hawsers ready for mooring. Soon they secure alongside a quay with tall cranes towering above the boat and the party of prisoners are led across the gangplank and loaded into a grey truck for their journey to Rouen. Unescorted, the truck bumps out of the dockyard, threads its way through the dingy streets until it reaches the main road to Caen and Rouen, and picks up speed.

*

The Colonel and his gang are at a loss. They have been disowned by the more legitimate partisan groups and the Allies, who have come to realise they are no more than a bunch of opportunists who cannot be relied upon to carry out even the most mundane of tasks. So they have not received supplies or ammunition from air-drops and know little of what goes on about them. They must scavenge about the countryside to survive, and become the scourge of local farmers and isolated house-holders, who will think nothing of reporting their activities to the Germans just to be rid of them. With ammunition running low, and food supplies difficult to obtain, it is decided to stick their necks out and ambush an enemy truck or two. Perhaps if they restrict their raids to Germans they will gain a molecule of respect from the local community.

It is not easy to waylay a military truck though, for they travel in convoy along the main road. So, when the lorry carrying the British prisoners diverts at Bayeux to take the minor road leading north through Douvres, it falls right into the laps of the Colonel's men as they lie in wait for just such a piece of good fortune.

Six

The executions have had a profound effect on the village, for a wedge has been driven between those who collaborate with the Germans and those who do not. There is a growing tension too as the threat of invasion becomes the main topic of conversation amongst the inhabitants as they watch the troops become more jumpy. They are 'stood to' for much of the time, and no longer venture out of their barracks without weapons, while Müller's Panthers take up carefully prepared positions with elaborate camouflage at strategic points along the road leading out to the headland, and one of Etienne's friends comes in to complain bitterly of the way the SS have driven a tank right into one of his barns while he was milking, knocking one wall down and sticking its long gun-barrel through the window facing the cross-roads just below his house.

More defensive positions are being set up round the village and more restrictions imposed on the villagers, until it is as though they are in a state of siege. Rumour is rife as stories of increased partisan activity and sabotage filter in from outside, and there are no trains in or out of Caen now as the Allied airforces bomb the stations and junctions, so that transport is completely disrupted everywhere and the roads clogged with military traffic. Suspicion between occupied and occupier grows as itchy-fingered SS troopers patrol the street, watching every move, so that just to venture out is an ordeal, and everyone becomes furtive in their efforts to remain unobtrusive.

In the Martin household there is a dramatic change too, for

there is a new set to Etienne's jaw, and he no longer scurries to obey his wife's scathing orders. Nicole notices a difference in her mother's attitude also, a strange expression in the way she looks at him. Not respect perhaps, but neither is it the usual offhand disdain. Potter is confined to his attic bedroom where he holds boredom at bay by working on a map of the area, and plotting details of the defences as supplied by Nicole and Etienne. He has no idea what use they might serve, but it is a means of passing the long hours while he waits for them to decide what to do with him.

Dupont loses much of his bluster as the villagers take on a new attitude towards him and the small group of 'elders' who purport to run their affairs. He finds himself openly snubbed by most, and the respect they once showed has turned to hostility. He no longer dominates the meetings, and the final outrage occurs when Etienne, the ever-faithful, tells him to 'shut up' in the middle of one of his rambling orations, and when he looks to the others for support he finds nothing but contempt as they all seek to make plain their new image to the world.

In many ways he is more honest than they, for he refuses to change his ways one iota. He sees no wrong in fraternising with the Germans while they are the governing authority, thus ensuring that the affairs of the village roll on smoothly. There will be time enough to come to a new arrangement if and when the Allies come. Until then it is essential that rules are obeyed and they treat the occupation forces with respect. When one of the conseillers refers to the hangings as an atrocity he takes him to task for using ill-considered language that might stir up trouble if less responsible people heard what was being said. The Germans are fighting a war he maintains, and they cannot afford to allow subversive elements to stab them in the back. He has no doubt that the Allies will deal with saboteurs in the same manner.

When he returns home he finds Petra, his Doberman bitch, stretched out on his doorstep with her throat cut, and excrement stuffed through his letter-box, while inside his family cower amongst broken glass as the wind whines through the broken panes of his windows.

Outraged, he goes straight to Hauptmann Becq's headquarters to complain, demanding that a guard be put on his property immediately, only to find the officer overwhelmed with an influx of emergency orders, with no time to spare for the expostulations of this supercilious oaf. The conseiller is taken completely aback when, after putting up with his tirade for almost five minutes, the Hauptmann swings on him and shouts, 'Get out of my office at once, you overstuffed turkey! I have no time for your nonsense.' He strides towards Dupont, forcing him back towards the open door. 'A few broken windows! Shit stuffed through your letter-box! Don't you know what is going on, you old fool!'

Absolutely deflated, Dupont staggers out into the street where insolent villagers are highly amused at his humiliation, and laugh outright at his embarrassment. Bewildered, rejected, he weaves his way back home, ignoring the frightened faces of his simpering wife and his anaemic daughter, to go straight into his study. Here too the square-paned windows are shattered and glass crunches beneath his feet as he walks across the rich carpet to pull the bell-rope for Henri. After a moment the old servant slithers through the door with his grey head even more bowed than usual on his stooping, narrow shoulders. The skin is like parchment on his skull of a face, while shadows emphasize his deep, sunken eyes, as he stands wavering on his stork-legs.

'Cognac!' growls Dupont. 'And send Emile to me. We will have to do something about these windows.'

'Emile has gone, sir. Everyone has gone.' The dull, colourless tone is like the sound of death. He holds the decanter in one claw while he summons up courage to say, 'I would like to go home to my family, sir. They say there has been bombing at Caen, and I would like to see if they are all right.' With difficulty he controls his shaking talons to pour out a measure for his master.

'Your family,' grumbles Dupont. 'I didn't know you had a

family.' He looks up with suspicion. 'You never bothered with them before, and I have not seen them visit you here. Why this concern all of a sudden?'

For the first time the old eyes look up at him. In the dull light the servant looks incredibly ancient, like a piece of antique furniture, eaten away with woodworm. 'I wish to be with them, sir. My sister and her children are alone since my brother-in-law was killed. I do not think they should be alone at such a time.'

'What are you babbling about?' He drains his cognac in one gulp. 'What on earth do you expect to happen?'

'They say there is to be an invasion, sir. We are very near the coast. Perhaps it would be prudent for all the household to evacuate.'

Dupont stands up to tower over his servant. 'I cannot spare you. As for moving away, that is stupid talk. Do you really believe that the Allies will come to this God-forsaken coast when the Pas-de-Calais is only a quarter of the distance? Do you think they will want to scramble through the Bocage where even the farmers curse the hedgerows and the earthbanks when they try to plough? Think of the swamps, man. They would be crazy to try such a venture. As for your family, they have looked after themselves and ignored you for so long you can have no obligations there. Your duty is to me and my family. Don't be scared, Henri. Believe me, a few broken windows and that filth on the doorstep is only the act of cowardly vandals. There is no need to run away from the likes of them.'

Henri lifts his eyes to stare mournfully at his master. 'I have no fear, sir. I just do not want to serve you any longer. I watched those men die without dignity or prayer and saw German officers standing with their soldiers. Then remembered how I have served them with wine at your table, taken their caps at your door and listened to them giving you your orders. I do not wish to be in your house any more.' He sets the decanter down on the platter, running his parchment fingers over the fine lead crystal as though savouring the last memory of an old world.

Dupont watches the frail old bag of bones pull open the heavy door and close it carefully behind him. His footsteps shuffle through the hall, and then he comes into view again, walking with his shoulders hunched under his wide-brimmed black hat as he goes towards the gate. The conseiller chokes back the hard lump in his throat and finds his anger replaced by a great sadness. The house is cold, and although he has never felt need of friendship he suddenly feels terribly alone.

*

Etienne watches the German trucks thundering through the village with helmeted soldiers seated upright on the wooden bench seats, the whole scene has changed in the past two days. The regular habits of the garrison as they go about the village performing the many mundane duties concerned with the everyday catering for the troops has been replaced by a new, purposeful era. They are never without their rifles and seem to come under the control of Müller's SS.

He sees Henri wandering slowly down the street towards the bridge in his dark clothes and suddenly realises that he has never seen him in sunlight before. The old retainer seemed to be part of the fixtures and fittings of the Dupont household, and now there is grey dust settling on his heavy greatcoat, and the wind moulds his drainpipe trousers to his thin legs. He is like the angel of death walking through the village, an intrusion on the faded pastel shades of the street. Black, like a raven, he drifts along with his bony legs tottering on the uneven flagstones of the pavement.

Marcel's lorry comes up the street from the bridge. Slotted between the grey military vehicles it reaches the cobbled fore-court in front of Etienne's shop, where it pulls off the road and parks under the elms. The driver's door creaks open and Marcel climbs down from his cab to walk deliberately towards Etienne's house. Once inside he wastes no time with formalities. It is as though he hasn't a second to spare. 'Etienne, I must speak to Nicole and the airman: it is most important.'

Without replying Etienne nods and leads the way towards the stairs. 'Fetch Nicole,' he tells his wife, and it is a sign of the times that she immediately drops her ladle and scurries off to do his bidding.

In the attic Potter is waiting, impatient and bored with his confinement. He looks up hopefully when he sees the lorry driver enter. '*Bonjour, Marcel,*' he grins. 'Have you found a way to get me back home?'

The Frenchman's face is serious. '*Non, monsieur.* There is no way back home for you.' He makes no attempt to explain until Etienne and Nicole arrive.

'What is it, Marcel?' she demands tersely. 'You know very well you should not come here like this.'

He ignores her. 'Was your ship called *Cyclops*?' he asks Potter.

'*Is* called *Cyclops*,' corrects the pilot.

'*Non, monsieur – was.* I have to tell you that she was sunk two days ago, and the Colonel has some of her sailors with his group.'

'Sunk!' exclaims Potter incredulously. 'I can't believe it!'

'She was attacked by the Luftwaffe, torpedoed and sent to the bottom – there is no mistake. The sailors say many more were picked up by a destroyer, but a lot died also.' He hesitates when he sees the shock register on Potter's face, then goes on, 'The Colonel wishes to meet you as soon as possible.'

'What for?' interrupts Nicole sharply. 'Do not trust him, monsieur. The Colonel and his gang are no more than a bunch of petty thieves. They have nothing to do with the real Maquisard.'

'That is the reason he wishes to talk,' he snaps. 'You do not know what you are talking about, Nicole.'

'How would we get there?' asks Potter.

'You don't – I bring him here.'

'Here!' exclaims Etienne. 'You cannot bring him to this house!'

'That's right, we cannot,' agrees Marcel smugly. 'We are going to bring him and the Englishmen to the house of

Dupont, the conseiller.' He grins at their vague expressions. 'Believe me, the arrangements have all been made. Dupont and his family are on their own in the big house; we have seen to that. There are no servants and all his German friends are much too busy for social calls. The enemy will not bother to watch his house too closely; what happened there today leaves no doubt about whose side he is on. He and many others are about to get their well-earned deserts: you have just about crawled out of the barrel, Etienne,' he sneers.

Etienne's eyes narrow. 'Don't pontificate with me, Marcel. No one is fooled by your pretences. I don't know your so-called Colonel, but I do know the type of scoundrel you are, and those with whom you associate. So, don't play the patriotic partisan with me.'

'Stop it, you two!' Nicole places herself between them. 'How do we get to the house?'

'Simple. No one will think twice if Etienne makes a call. After all.' he leers, 'they have been bosom pals for long enough. It will be quite natural for you to accompany your father. I'll get the pilot to the house. Here!' He passes a rolled-up set of mechanic's overalls. 'Put these on, and when we get to my truck, crawl underneath and pretend you are fixing something.' He turns to Etienne gloatingly. 'We have a special little job for you too, Monsieur Martin. It will prove how much of a reformed character you are.'

*

In the big house the Dupont family sit eating a meal cooked by Madam Dupont. It is nothing like the lavish spread that usually graces their table even in these austere times, for although there are shortages in the cities and in Germany both villagers and occupiers have never gone short. Dupont himself has blocked off the worst of the broken windows with make-shift boarding, newspapers and cushions, for it is too late to get anyone in for proper repairs, but he has no doubt that tomorrow when things have got back into order again it will all be attended to.

The food, and in particular the wine make him feel a lot better. A few vandals with brains no larger than peanuts will not deter him from his duties to the community. He will call a meeting and tell the idiots what must be done to ensure the village lives through this small crisis. The main thing is to regain normality; to carry on in such a way that will assuage the Germans to the extent that they will realise there is no threat from the locals. If and when the Allies arrive he and his small group of dignitaries will meet them as they did the Germans, to negotiate a satisfactory agreement whereby the villagers will continue their rural activities in a civilised manner, and not interfere with the military. That way the war will pass them by, and those who have brains enough will congratulate him and his colleagues for the stability of village life throughout it all. There might even come a time when the square will be graced by a statue of Monsieur Dupont, the man who led them through the turmoil with dignity and sanity. He wipes his mouth and reaches for the cheese. After the meal he will enjoy a glass or two of calvados alone in his study. He has quite a speech to compose for tomorrow's meeting.

'It is Etienne Martin!' exclaims Monique, breaking into his thoughts, 'and he has Nicole with him.'

Sure enough the insignificant little wretch is tottering up the drive with his daughter. Whenever Dupont sees the vivacious firebrand he is struck by the irony of Etienne producing such a girl while his own Monique is such a simpering introvert. Though when he looks at his wife he is not so surprised. The astonishing thing is that they have managed to produce anything at all between them.

'So!' he breathes with heavy satisfaction. 'Already the sheep are returning to the fold. You will have to answer the door, woman,' he orders. 'I will see Etienne in my study, and while he is with me I do not wish to be interrupted. I have a thing or two to say to him. You can keep Nicole amused with Monique: take her into the parlour.' He is quite prepared to be magnanimous after he has put Etienne in his place, and he takes his stance near the marble mantelpiece with a benign smile on his face.

He almost drops his glass when the door bursts open and they both stride in through Madame's protests without any attempt at propriety. There is no change at all in the abrasive manners of the bicycle seller, and he seems to bristle with his new-found bumptiousness as he faces up to his old lord and master. 'I have come to arrange an emergency meeting, Dupont. Will ten thirty suit you?'

'You arrange a meeting!' gasps the conseiller. 'Since when did you take it upon yourself to arrange meetings?'

Before Etienne can answer the door bursts open once more and Marcel is there with Potter. This time Dupont is lost for words as he stares with shocked eyes into the barrel of a luger. 'Go and fetch Madame and Monique,' says Marcel quietly to Nicole. 'As for you, conseiller, for the first time in your life you are going to be of some use to us. These are to be our headquarters.'

*

Events seem to have passed like a dream for Mort. The period in the U-boat did not allow much rest after their ordeal, and that has been followed by a jolting, stop-start drive in the back of the German army truck with two stone-faced guards sitting bolt upright by the tail-board, while their sergeant – the only one with a smattering of English – rides in the cab with the driver. They make slow progress in a column of traffic until their lorry turns off to the left into a country lane and builds up speed for a while as they rumble through small clutches of Norman houses and patchwork countryside. Each time one of them attempts to speak one of the guards barks a rebuke and rattles his rifle bolt, so they settle back to while away the time as they journey north-east.

Mort shakes himself out of a half-doze when the truck slows down to walking pace. There is a small gap in the canvas hood through which it is possible to see an old horse-drawn wagon straddling the lane with its load of brassicas. The driver is hunched behind the undulating rump of his horse making no attempt to move over to the side of the road, and seems oblivious to the angry shouts of the sergeant. Even tooting the horn has no effect as the driver tries to get past. The cart stays stubbornly in the centre of the lane until it reaches the muddy gate of a farm where it comes to a halt while the driver climbs stiffly from his seat to go to the horse's head, for the narrow gate has to be negotiated with the utmost care. It is as though the Germans do not exist and they fume as he meticulously pushes the gate to its widest extent and ambles back to take hold of the reins. The old nag should have been taken to the knacker's yard long ago, but it stumps its clumsy hooves into the mud as its master lines it up with the entrance.

Suddenly strident shouts destroy the pastoral scene, and several villainous looking men clamber into the truck, waving an assortment of weapons and shouting, '*Allez! Allez!*' The British seamen join their guards with hands clasped on their heads as they spill over the tail-board to be bundled unceremoniously into the farm. Behind them the truck's engine revs up and its wheels come splashing and slipping behind them. They are lined up against a wall inside one of the outbuildings where outraged chickens flutter away from a forest of moving legs, while excited Frenchmen search everyone's clothing.

They are made to stand in the dim light while a heated discussion takes place as the partisans examine their trophies. In the midst of it all the Colonel arrives, and after a great deal of shouting and argument, manages to restore some semblance of order. They drag the Germans away to a remote corner of the barn, and then he directs his attention to Mort and the others.

'Where do you come from?' he asks in good English.

It takes time to explain, and while they try there are the sounds of a struggle from the dark recesses of the barn, followed by heavy breathing and then silence. Several of the Colonel's men return with grins on their faces as they wipe the blades of a selection of knives. Further argument takes place before a man is sent off with a message, and the seamen are loaded back into the truck with some of the French dressed in

German uniforms to 'guard' them.

It is growing dark when they rumble into the village and through the gates of Dupont's house. The conseiller suddenly finds himself host to a rabble of unwelcome guests who take over the whole place and ransack his possessions like a swarm of locusts. They rampage through the building, scuffling and arguing over their finds. Completely out of control, they loot and destroy everything in sight until they are satisfied that they have searched through the whole house, and look about for more mischief. Monique finds herself the centre of attraction for a crowd of lechers whose lewd comments and suggestions teach her more about the facts of life in five minutes than she would learn in a lifetime in her sheltered environment.

'Disciplined mob, ain't they?' comments Envoldsen as a particularly loud bang shakes the house.

'Regular bunch of choir-boys,' says Mort. He has been staring at Potter with a curious expression. 'Where do you reckon he got that watch? That's naval issue if I ever saw one.'

'You're absolutely correct.' Potter's upper class accent takes them all by surprise. 'I am Lieutenant-Commander Potter, a Corsair pilot from *Cyclops*. Who are you?'

Envoldsen takes care of the introductions while the French look on curiously from the sidelines, and in the midst of it all one of the Flouquet brothers comes in.

'We want Dupont,' he demands.

The Colonel's hold over the gang is tenuous. The Flouquet brothers are supposed to be his lieutenants, but in reality they allow him to play the leader only because it suits them to do so, for he is the one member of the group with no criminal background, and they need him to bring an air of respectability to their exploits. The ambush was a dead loss as far as they are concerned, although the contraband from this house has made up for it in some measure. They are beyond his control in their treatment of prisoners, and although he is a hardened soldier, some of the acts of bestiality they perform make him cringe. He knows their evening will not be complete without a game with the Duponts and he would like to keep the conseiller.

'He is too important,' he insists. 'We must have him.'

Eugene Flouquet glowers at him. 'That swine above all others we must have, Colonel. Do not try to keep him from us.'

This confrontation has been brewing for some time. The Colonel's credibility has gradually slipped away now that he can no longer obtain arms and supplies from official sources. He knows they no longer need him and find his everlasting condemnation of their behaviour a bit of a bind. It is for this reason that he has planned a meeting with the English officer. After today the gang can go its own way, and good riddance, as far as he is concerned. First, however, he needs Dupont. The conseiller has hobnobbed with the enemy for so long that he must have vital information, and can probably be used in other ways.

'Take the two women,' he hears himself saying. 'Put them in the truck and take them away.'

'No!' screams Dupont, shaking with fear and rage. 'You cannot allow these animals to take them.'

The renegades who have squeezed through the doorway are delighted. Pierre La Salle, the pig breeder who was caught in one of his own sties with the ten-year-old daughter of a neighbour is almost slavering. 'Sounds good to me,' he grates, with his watery eyes fixed on the two cowering women.

Eugene is not convinced. 'What will you do when he has served his purpose?'

'Hand him over to the authorities. He will be tried like the rest of the war criminals.'

'Oh no! That is not enough. He belongs to the village and his punishment must be witnessed by everyone.'

'All right, all right!' sighs the Colonel. 'I will promise to hand him over to you afterwards.'

'When?'

'A week – no more.'

They eye each other for a moment, but the remainder are getting restless. 'All right,' agrees Eugene. 'In one week he is ours. In the meantime, you fat bastard!' he spits into Dupont's face. 'Use your imagination. These lads have some very funny habits. Your wife and daughter are going to have the time of their lives.'

Potter will never forget the expressions on the women's faces as they are dragged out. They do not struggle, but stare beseechingly at those who stand helplessly aside. After the noise has died away he turns to the Colonel. 'You are as bad as the Germans.'

'Perhaps,' agrees the Colonel sadly. 'I too would like to fight a nice clean war and abide by the chivalrous rules of combat, but I have to live with reality. Perhaps now that you have come down out of the clouds you will see the mud and grime like we do. However, I am sick of trying to turn that bunch into a fighting force. Just once I would like to do something that will hurt the Germans and help in the battle to free my poor country. So I come to you, for you are the only professionals I know who will have anything to do with me.'

'Professionals!' scoffs Potter. 'I am a flier, and these men are seamen. What do we know of guerrilla warfare?'

'At least you are disciplined – you don't know how much I yearn for discipline. There must be a target worth going for. Everyone knows the invasion will come soon, and the FFI are fighting quite openly already. The more Germans we keep chasing after us the fewer there will be to meet the Allies when they invade.'

'The only target I know of is the radar station, and we have already destroyed that,' states Potter.

'No you did not,' declares Nicole. 'You destroyed only a decoy.'

The four seamen are at a loss to understand what is going on, for the talk is all in French and they are left to sit like little boys at a grown-up tea party while the discourse flows to and fro. Marcel listens with half an ear, but his attention is focused mainly on the conseiller, while Etienne flaps about on the fringe.

'What about some grub?' asks Mort suddenly. 'There must be something worth eating somewhere,' and he and Wordsley wander through the ransacked house until they find the kitchen. The partisans have helped themselves here too, but they find enough cheese and bread to satisfy their hunger, and a couple of jars of French cider completes the picnic. When they return the discussion is at an end, and once the food is shared out Potter takes the seamen to one side to explain the radar and the Colonel's proposal.

'It is up to you before we go any further,' he tells them. 'As I see it we have three alternatives: one, to lie low until the Allies reach us; God only knows when that will be. Two, give ourselves up to the Germans and spend the rest of the war in a POW camp – if we are lucky. Three, have a go at doing something to help the war effort. I have no need to explain that if we are caught in those circumstances it is no use quoting the Geneva Convention.'

'Sod that!' explodes Malloy. 'I'm a bleedin' matelot; not a half-hard pongo, runnin' rahned with a lot of froggies with a flamin' bird-man in charge. Yer can count me out, mate, and there's nuffin' yer can do abaht it.'

'Stow it, Malloy,' barks Envoldsen. He looks seriously at Potter. 'What are we gettin' ourselves into with this lot, sir? Judgin' by what I've seen, they're about as organised as a piss-up in a brewery.'

Potter sighs and sits back. 'I must admit they don't inspire me with confidence, but the girl seems genuine enough, and her father – the one with the chins – is itching to have a go at the Germans. It seems they have done something that has really upset him. We have not discussed a plan yet, I wouldn't do that until I know what you think.'

'I'm giving myself up to no bastard German!' states Mort firmly. 'We pissed about on that Jonah of a carrier for long enough with nothing to show for our efforts. I don't know what the others think, but if the bloody Jerries want me they're gonna have to find me.' He looks directly into Potter's eyes. 'Nor am I gonna get mixed up with any daft schemes with these murdering bastards – sir.'

Wordsley pipes up. 'I reckon we'll be in dead trouble even if we do give ourselves up. I wouldn't like to try and explain that we are only with these blokes by accident.'

It is a sobering thought, and even Malloy has to agree with it. When they break down the alternatives they realise there is not a great deal of choice. Either they surrender and risk being shot as saboteurs, or they put themselves in the Colonel's hands, for to survive in occupied France they will need help.

*

Müller is with the Hauptmann when the signal comes in about a missing truck in their area with its cargo of prisoners and escort. He spends much of his time with Becq in the command bunker on the headland, and each time the big Würzburg picks up a contact he becomes engrossed with the fire-drill as the two big 21cm batteries go into action. Inside the cabin naval operators study their display tubes, passing accurate ranges and bearings to the command centre, working in tandem with the Lietstand optical range-finder. The major is there purely as an observer, for it is through these electronic marvels that the first sign of an invading fleet will be seen, and although he is still convinced that the Pas-de-Calais is the most likely place for the landings, there is always an outside chance of something big happening here. He is fascinated by the technology as the details are fed into the instruments to be analysed for the big guns. The operators with headphones clamped to their skulls are expert as they calculate trajectory, wind-speed, even air temperature, so that the projectiles soar into the stratosphere and fall with precision onto targets up to nineteen kilometres away.

Today, however, except for a series of anti-aircraft warnings the world seems to be holding its breath, and the big guns stay silent. So there is time to study the signal, measure its contents and exercise his mind with its implications. The last known position of the truck is where it diverted from the main road onto the north route, for it fuelled at the dump near Bayeux, and if it had continued along the main road it would have become jammed in the bottleneck further down, where right now marshals are trying to sort out the mess before daylight brings the RAF down on them. He draws a ten-kilometre circle round the area, and it encompasses the village and the farm where they found the deserter. He is certain there is a band of partisans in the district, and this is just the kind of thing they would relish: a lone truck, probably loaded with arms and supplies, weaving slowly through country lanes would make a tempting target. If he moves quickly now he can throw a cordon round the whole area before morning, and then he will tighten the noose until he finds his quarry.

'Hauptmann Becq!'

When Becq hears what he has in mind he agrees to spare some of his own men and trucks, if only to keep Müller out of his hair for a while.

From his perch high up on the ruined abbey the partisan lookout stretches his muscles as the sun pokes its head over the treetops to the east to look out across the valley, and what he sees sends him diving for cover beneath the wall, for there are army vehicles moving into position to block the roads leading to the hide-out while grey figures move in across the fields. He leaves his post to race down to the farm where the truck stands draped in a camouflage of branches and bracken.

The Flouquet brothers roust out the blurry-eyed partisans who are feeling the effects of large quantities of Dupont's wine and spirits after a long night's orgy with their two captives. Now they scamper about in panic with no-one in command and no set pattern of defence. The ominous sound of metal tracks and the sharp snap of orders seem to come from all directions. They have no place to run and they know full well what lies in store for them if they are captured, so they scratch about for every semblance of cover and weld their quaking bodies into the ground as though mother earth will keep them safely tucked into her bosom. Their sweaty hands clamp hard on their weapons while the ring of professional soldiers closes in on them.

Eugene looks about at his disoriented men as they shift from one place to another. They have been transformed into terrified individuals, each scratching about for somewhere to hide from the menacing noise of approaching armour. The very air vibrates about them, and they look round for someone to take the lead. He needs to make a decision, find a rallying point to regain them some semblance of order.

'The Abbey!' he shouts at them, pointing urgently up the hill. 'The Abbey! We will be on the high ground there, and we can use the walls as a fort!' His brother and a few of the more stable members of the gang badger the others up the slope towards the ruins. Now he has them concentrated in a defensive position where he can keep an eye on them he feels better. The high ground, that is what the Colonel always insisted upon. 'Gain the high ground,' he would say, 'and you hold the advantage.' Eugene is not to know that the Colonel's tactics are from another war.

Müller smiles when one of his troopers reports the partisans taking up their new positions on the hillock amongst the crumbling ruins, for it will be much easier to take care of them now than it would have been to weed them out of every nook and cranny of the sprawling farm.

'Tell Schultz to bring up his Nebelwerfer,' he orders, then turns to one of the Wehrmacht sergeants. 'And you – you have mortars?'

The man snaps to attention. 'Yes, Herr Major, we have four.'

'Good! We will have ourselves a little competition – your Granatwerfer 34s against our rocket-launcher. I want those peasants eliminated.'

The nervous partisans crouch behind their walls with their insides churning as the engines die and nature takes over with her gentle sounds.

'Wait until you can see them,' orders Eugene in a hoarse whisper. 'Don't give your positions away.'

The sun is well up over the horizon; soaking up moisture from the granite walls and warming their anxious faces. High in the sky the steady drone of aircraft sounds a million miles away and one youngster releases his pent-up breath with a whimper. They can hear the clink and rattle of war machinery and the strident orders coming closer on the thin air, and they grip their puny weapons more tightly as they watch every shadow for the first sign of the advancing enemy.

The mortar shells burst with appalling detonation right in amongst them, and before they can recover from the shock others explode in a relentless bombardment that grinds into their skulls like a drill to send them cringing into huddled bundles of cringing flesh and bone. Someone screams a thin, transparent sound amid the violent percussions that destroy the mind, and jumps up to run wide-eyed across the smoke-filled enclosure, croaking incoherent sounds as the world is torn apart about him, waving his arms wildly above his head until he reaches the arch where his croaks are cut off abruptly when bullets thud into his soft chest from carefully concealed snipers.

Now come the rockets. 'Moaning Minnies', the British call them, and they streak in with fiery tails to pulverise the area, and the noise is unbelievable. Each time someone tries to make a break he is brought down by a fusillade of concentrated fire. They are like rabbits scurrying from a smoke-filled warren as bodies are tossed into the air or shattered where they lie. The wounded try to crawl into shelter, only to be blown apart by another shell as the whole arena is methodically cratered metre by metre, and the ruined walls are reduced to piles of smoking rubble, with bloody limbs poking out from underneath.

'Cease fire!' orders Müller, and the cacophony subsides.

The hill looks like a volcano with a pall of dust and smoke rising from the mess of bodies and stone. The whole countryside is shocked into silence, but gradually begins to come alive again with cautious rustles and tentative chirrups. Müller's men creep out, bending low as they weave in short runs while their comrades cover them. He is proud of his troopers as they move in like well-oiled machines with only the occasional grunt from an NCO to guide them. When they reach their objective they find no threat, only a pathetic array of twisted bodies. Incredibly a limb stirs here and there, and a strangled groan escapes from a dust-filled mouth, but the wounded are despatched by cold-eyed marksmen as though they are culling surplus wild-stock.

Satisfied with his handiwork Müller turns his attention to the farm. It looks deceptively quiet and peaceful as they move in towards the buildings. The windows are dusty and lifeless in their dingy sockets, and the troops creep in closer to divide into separate squads and infiltrate the outhouses. At last only the main farmhouse remains, and while infantrymen move round to the rear the armoured cars move in until the place is encircled with a ring of steel. Müller is with his own men, crouched behind a low wall that runs round the perimeter of a squalid yard with piles of manure and thick mud encroaching from every corner. The door is slightly ajar and no sound or movement comes from within. A sergeant snaps a curt order and two troopers advance, keeping low, weaving from side to side until they flatten against the farmhouse wall. Each one carries a sub-machine gun, and one man unclips a grenade from his shoulder-strap and primes it. He nods to his mate, and in one combined movement the door is kicked open and the grenade hurled into the gloomy passage beyond. Before the dust settles they are inside, spraying bullets in all directions, while the remainder of Müller's men charge across the yard.

After a time an upstairs window is thrust open and one of his sergeants is there, leaning out to request that the major come to look at what they have discovered. He is met at the door and led upstairs to a door that opens into one of the bedrooms where Monique cringes in a corner, nude, blubbering, and staring with shocked eyes at her mother stretched across the bed also naked, with her body bruised and scarred by dozens of cigarette burns. Her hands and feet are tied to the bedposts and she stares wildly from face to face with a crazed expression while they crowd in on her. Müller looks down at her for a moment as she struggles for breath with blood streaming from her mouth and nostrils, then stumps out into the fresh air again.

'The Wehrmacht will take care of them,' he grunts. 'Let us get back to our vehicles.'

'Sir!' A corporal comes running from the house to stand

rigid in front of Müller; he is one of the Hauptmann's men.

'Well?'

'Sir, they are the wife and daughter of Monsieur Dupont, the conseiller. He has always been helpful to us and worked closely with the Hauptmann.'

'So!' He takes a couple of thoughtful paces. 'Is that the missing truck?' He points to a small section of tailboard that shows beyond the corner of the house.

'Yes, sir.'

'Very well. You will place the two women in that truck and lead my scout-car to the home of Monsieur Dupont. Send someone else to tell Hauptmann Becq what has occurred here. Perhaps then we can clear this tangle.'

He strides to his vehicle and sits waiting while the women are bundled into blankets and carried to the lorry. The infantry are forming up and marching away to their barracks, and the lorries roar up the lane towards the main road in clouds of dust. Müller's driver stays twenty metres behind the lorry as they head for Dupont's home. A mottled brown and white cow ambles curiously into the yard chewing the cud and gazing about her with baleful eyes. She lumbers across to the open door and blunders into the passage. Her mournful bellow punctuates the episode.

Seven

It has been a fitful night as they tried to snatch periods of sleep while taking turns to keep watch and stand guard over the conseiller. Not that he required much attention, for he has remained in his chair throughout the long hours without moving; just staring vacantly into space. Dawn arrives without anyone realising it, for the blackouts are solid and they are taken by surprise when someone takes them down and allows pale light to invade the stagnant atmosphere of the study to emphasize the drabness of the furniture. Marcel and Etienne smoked pungent cigarettes most of the time and when Mort opens the big windows the fresh, morning air wafts in like a tonic.

There are already people moving about the village, for curfew ends at six a.m. and soon tradesmen will call, or the first inquisitive passer-by will stop to take a closer look at the broken windows, perhaps even come in through the gate to investigate. Word will get about that there is something unusual going on at the Dupont house, and suspicions will be roused.

'That radar station must be worth going for,' Potter's voice rises above the subdued murmur of conversation. 'The Navy doesn't waste aircraft on worthless targets.'

'Is there a way of getting to it?' asks Mort, and Potter lapses into French as he talks to the Colonel and Nicole. 'It will not be easy,' he says at last. 'The whole headland is out of bounds and the station is almost at the cliff-edge. The area is a mass of gun-emplacements and bunkers. However, the girl has come up with an idea, though the Colonel doesn't give it much chance. In fact I have to tell you that as far as he is concerned she is a hot-head with no regard for her own or anyone else's safety. His advice is not to touch any of her mad-cap ideas.'

'You don't sound too convinced, sir,' says Mort.

'I reckon half a chance is all you get when you plan something like this. Sometimes the more audacious a scheme, the better it works.' He shrugs his shoulders. 'I'll explain for what it is worth. It seems the local big-wig goes up to his command bunker every day in his commandeered Citroen. The sentries on the barrier always search his car thoroughly before it is allowed into the restricted zone, for he has a thing about being not treated any differently to anyone else. The Colonel would create a diversion which could get us through the barbed wire.'

'Oh great!' scoffs Wally. 'It's us against the whole German army.'

Ignoring him, Potter goes on: 'This chap' – he indicates Dupont – 'is a great friend of the Germans. That's why he is so popular with the natives, as you may have noticed. Nicole reckons that if the Colonel promises to restore his wife and daughter relatively undamaged, and guarantee his own safety when our blokes come, he will play ball.'

'And do what?' asks Mort.

'That comes later. First we have to get the head man to call on us with his posh Citroen.'

'Phew!' breathes Envoldsen. 'That's a bit iffy! Look at 'im. 'E ain't said a word or stirred since last night, not even ter 'ave a piss. Can't imagine 'im convincin' anyone, let alone a German officer.'

'It won't be him,' says Potter. 'The girl's father will do the convincing. I don't know the ins and outs of it, but it seems that until yesterday they were bosom pals, and the Germans think he is Dupont's little doggy. The bossman is a regular visitor to this house so he won't be too surprised to be asked to call.' He sighs wearily. 'I don't know; maybe it is all a bit of a bloody nonsense. We're not commandos after all: but we are already in it up to the hilt anyway, and we can't stay here doing nothing.'

'Blimey!' snarls Malloy, who has listened with only half an ear as he stands by the window. 'Listen ter this lot!'

They stop talking and the reverberations of a bombardment shake the old house. It is continuous, like a distant thunderstorm, and it goes on for some time, painting graphic pictures in their minds. When it ceases the silence that follows is even more nerve-racking, and no-one attempts to offer a guess at what it means, but with one accord they determine to stay in the village no longer than absolutely necessary.

Etienne leaves the house on his own; surprised that he is so calm in the circumstances. He is aglow with his new-found self-confidence, having set aside the timorous role he played for so long and assumed this new strength of character as though it is something he has sought after all his life without realising it existed. He doesn't hesitate as he strides up to the Hauptmann's office. The big Citroen is parked waiting and its driver lounges with a couple of soldiers, staring towards the east where the sounds of the bombardment came from. They are the nervous ones now. He can see it in their faces as they look up into the sky. The sky and the sea hold menace for them, and on all fronts to east and south their comrades are falling back to the fatherland, and soon their time will come. He gloats on their anxiety as he nods greeting to the driver who knows him well. Even the sentry looks uneasy as he allows the little man to enter.

Inside Becq is pulling on his highboots. He was at the command bunker until the early hours but feels fully alert and fresh this morning. He knows full well what the noise was, and hopes that Müller is enjoying himself with the partisans, for it keeps the arrogant major off his back. The thought improves his humour so that the appearance of Dupont's little toady can be tolerated. He regrets his abrasive manner yesterday, for they are going to need all the friends they can get in the next few weeks, and the conseiller, obnoxious though he is, has not faltered in his loyalty to the occupiers.

'Good morning, Monsieur Martin,' he greets in his perfect French. 'This is an early visit. You are just in time. I am about to leave for my bunker.'

'I was anxious to catch you before you left, Herr Hauptmann. I have an urgent message from Monsieur Dupont. His home has been attacked.'

'I know,' Becq interrupts. 'He came to tell me and I am afraid it was at an inopportune moment. I was less than courteous; for which I must apologise.'

Etienne smiles; it is becoming easier by the minute. 'He knows how busy you are, Herr Hauptmann. He is extremely distressed, but he has found a clue that tells him where the scum who perpetrated the crime are hiding, and there is every likelihood the British airman is there with them. He does not wish to leave his family this morning and asks if you will call at his house on your way to your duties.'

Becq stands and places a patronising hand on Etienne's shoulder. 'Of course. It is the least I can do, and you will ride with me.' It will be like putting one over on the major if he can find the airman. When they arrive he is shocked at the amount of damage to Dupont's house. Almost every window is smashed, and there is an air of dejection inside the gate. The conseiller has condemned himself in the eyes of the villagers for his collaboration. Etienne takes him straight through into the study where the Hauptmann is even more shocked at the change in Dupont. The conseiller's face is like putty. His lips tremble, and there is a haunted look in his eyes. Etienne has to urge him to speak, and when he does it is in a halting, disjointed patois that is almost impossible to understand, so Becq has to turn to Etienne for interpretation.

Outside the driver of the Citroen stretches his legs while he waits. The house is gloomy and the village sounds are screened by the trees and shrubs, making the garden a haven of silence. He tests each tyre with a kick then looks up to see Nicole emerge from the conservatory door near the corner of the house. She is struggling with a large bin, half dragging, half carrying it across the threshold. It is much too heavy for her to manage and a glance at the main door shows it firmly shut. So he goes across to her with an offer of help. His French is non-existent, but he places a hand on the bin and thumps his chest with an accompanying smile. She refuses to smile back and makes a further vain effort. Ignoring her protests he flexes his muscles and grabs both handles and lifts it chest high with remarkable ease. Reluctantly she points to a pile of rubbish at the far end of a long path. A look of uncertainty shadows his features for a second while he glances back towards the car, but all is quiet, and he follows the girl with the bin held high in front of him.

Marcel waits until they are well down the path before he creeps out of the bushes with a box and a length of wire. The box contains three British type grenades and a small quantity of soft explosive as supplied by the Colonel. He opens the boot-lid and places the box right forward under the back seat, then attaches the wire to the ring of a grenade before he threads it through the lock and secures it with difficulty to the latch on the lid while it is almost shut. He slips away before the driver returns to pace impatiently beside the car, cursing the time his master spends with Dupont. The hours he has spent waiting outside this house is shameful, and more often than not Becq comes out blurry-eyed and stinking of brandy.

Etienne emerges, followed by the Hauptmann with a bewildered expression on his face. He never imagined such a change could take place in a man. The conseiller was incapable of stringing two sentences together, and it had taken both of them a great deal of effort to extract any sense at all from his ramblings. Dupont muttered away in Norman patois and Etienne interpreted as best he could so that at least they were able to establish that the partisans were hiding at the farm and the pilot was there with them. This time he determines the Wehrmacht will do the job, and he can arrange it all from the bunker. Just once he would like to wipe the supercilious smile from the major's face.

Inside the house Marcel slips into the study where Dupont sits in a semi-trance with Etienne watching over him. Marcel moves behind the conseiller, pulls out a knife, and with one brief glance at Etienne slits Dupont's throat from ear to ear before thrusting him forward to bleed over the desk. For a moment Etienne is stunned as he listens to the gurgling noise and watches the twitchings of the slumped, obscene body, then he looks up at Marcel, sees the doubt in his eyes and grins.

'I think I could have done that,' he says evenly.

When the driver gets halfway back to his car Nicole moves in amongst the apple trees, watching carefully in case he should look back, but he is anxious to reach the car before the Hauptmann comes out, and she is able to melt into the orchard to break into a run towards the track that the Colonel will have taken when he led the English to the restricted area. She is determined to be with them when they cross over at the check-point despite their prejudices, for the Colonel made it quite plain that he did not wish her to accompany them. His excuse is that she cannot speak English and there must be no confusion when orders are given, but she knows the real reason and it serves to fortify her determination. She agreed to create this little diversion, and as far as they are concerned that is the end of her part in the affair. They couldn't be more wrong.

She has plenty of time, for Becq's car must go out on the highway some distance before turning into the minor road leading out to the headland. A hoarse, angry whisper brings her to where they are crouched amongst an outcrop of bare rock close to a path that descends to the beach. The area is dominated by two pill-boxes squatting each side of the road, guarding access to the point, and there is a barrier across the road where the sentries check every vehicle before it is allowed through. The gorse-strewn neck of the headland is under observation from the pill-boxes for a distance of fifty metres on either side, and beyond their range minefields guard the cliffs so well that it would be suicidal for anyone to try crossing that way. It all rests on the Colonel's diversion. When the explosion comes they must react without hesitation and get across no-man's-land into a gully that runs into a mass of undergrowth on the other side.

The Colonel's original plan was for only one or two of them to carry out the job with explosives, but Potter disagrees. Explosives will alert everyone, and the headland would be sealed off immediately, leaving no chance of escape. On the other hand, the Germans might think the booby-trapped Citroen is no more than an attempt on the Hauptmann's life, and Mort is convinced that if he can get into the control unit he can wreck the radar quite easily.

They settle for Potter's plan, and it means that everyone goes, armed with an assortment of weapons provided by the Colonel. No one pretends that when it comes to the test they will stand up to a squad of fully-trained soldiers. Stealth, surprise and the fact that the radar is operated by Naval non-combatants is in their favour, Potter assures them, and although there will probably be a sentry or two the Colonel reckons they can succeed if they do exactly as he says.

'Here it comes!' warns Envoldsen, and they switch their eyes to the road where the Hauptmann's car is approaching the checkpoint. Their nerves stretch taut as it slides to a halt and the sentries move out to check it.

'Christ!' exclaims Potter as they see Becq climb out of the car to speak with one of the guards. 'He has to choose today to break his routine!'

The tension mounts as they watch two of the sentries begin their search. Almost nonchalantly one of them goes to the rear and puts his hand on the boot-handle and twists it. The Colonel had hoped for a violent explosion and he is not disappointed, for the whole back-end of the car erupts in a sheet of flame, throwing the sentry across the road with the upper half of his body mangled into a bloody mess by flying metal and glass. Pieces of hardware rip into the other sentries as they dive for the ground while Becq is thrown off his feet and knocked unconscious. The men inside the pill-boxes stare wide-eyed at the carnage.

'Now!'

Potter's quiet command sets them running. Already the Germans are picking themselves up to shake sense back into their numbed brains as men rush out from the pill-boxes to aid the wounded. The driver is screaming for attention as he fights to free his trapped legs, very aware of flames licking round the petrol tank. One dedicated NCO is shouting to the pill-box crews to get back to their posts, concerned that the area is not being guarded, while a pall of black smoke rises over the scene as bodies are dragged hurriedly away from the fire. The tank explodes with a shattering roar, engulfing some of the would-be rescuers in flames, screaming and shouting as they try to beat out their flaming clothes. The Hauptmann struggles to his feet with blood running down his face, capless and with his uniform in tatters, as he strives to regain his senses in the midst of the smoke and turmoil.

The saboteurs get the few vital seconds they need to reach the gully unobserved, and when the noise subsides they are well into the restricted zone, moving in crouching runs through clumps of gorse where rabbit warrens abound. The Colonel leads them to an abandoned tin hut close to where the road branches into two small tracks. There they can have a breather and take stock of the situation.

'Hell! Where's Malloy?' Mort's startled voice sets them all looking round at the empty countryside. There is no sign of the AB.

'What now?' asks Envoldsen. 'That puts the muckers on everything, sir. I don't trust that useless bastard one inch. He'll shop us all to save his own skin.'

'Well we can't go back, that's for certain,' states Mort.

'Heh! Look! There it is!' Wordsley's excited shout interrupts them. He is staring through a gap in the corrugated iron. 'The radar aerial! It's there, only a couple of hundred yards away.'

Potter goes across with Mort. The iron is rusted in many places and they can look through the holes to see the big dish aerial with its camouflage of shrubbery intertwined in the mesh. It is mounted on a concrete blockhouse, and looms higher than the scattered pines standing sentinel on the cliff-edge.

'Look over there!' Mort points away to the left. 'That's a ship's range-finder if ever I saw one.' True enough, the familiar arms of a stereoscopic range-finder, festooned with camouflage netting and foliage, rises out of the ground like a giant mushroom with its domed cupola. There is at least ten metres between the bifocal lenses, and every seaman knows how the operator merges his twin images to gain accurate ranges on a target.

'The radar is more important,' states Mort firmly. 'They have to locate a target before they can use that, and that is where the radar comes in, for it will pick up a contact long before anyone sees it, even with the best binoculars in the world – especially when the visibility is bad.'

'Just think what that would mean if this is the spot where the invasion is to take place,' says Potter quietly. 'That thing could detect the ships long before they close in to the coast and give the enemy bags of time to organise his defences. A lot of men would die on the beaches.'

'You don't think they'll come here, do you, sir?' asks Envoldsen.

'It's a hell of a long way across, but the beaches are right for a landing, and if they are thinking of springing a surprise – why not?'

'If only we knew what that sod was up to,' grates Wally, bringing them down to earth with a bump.

'Yes,' agrees Potter. 'We were going to wait until dark, but if Malloy is trying to save his skin and ingratiate himself with the Germans, he could jeopardise the whole thing. Do you think we could do it in daylight?' he asks the Colonel.

'I don't know.' He is looking positively sick. 'I am cursed to work with amateurs. It is not only your man that worries me. What do we do with her?' He jabs a thumb at Nicole who is watching suspiciously. 'Speak French,' she says. 'If you are discussing me, speak French.'

'It is your own fault you are here. We have no time to bother with two languages.'

'All right! All right!' Potter tries to placate him. 'She is here and there is nothing we can do about it. She must know what is going on. We have argued long enough, especially if Malloy intends blowing the gaff. If it is at all possible I vote we go now.'

The Colonel looks round at their set faces and shakes his head gravely. 'We would not get twenty paces in daylight before they spot us. There is no choice but to wait until darkness. In the meantime we must study every inch of the terrain and plan our moves to the last second. Just pray hard that we may stay hidden until the time comes.'

'How long will that be?' grumbles Mort, looking up at the sun. 'The day has just started, and I keep thinking of that bastard running to the Germans. He could bring them down on us like a ton of bricks.'

*

Müller stalks about the study while his men carry out a search of the house. The conseiller's body is still slumped across the desk with his dead eyes staring at the telephone. Outside in the truck the two women are stretched out in their cocoons of bedding. Monique stares vacantly at the canvas roof while her mother, though much in pain from her numerous wounds, is awake and alive to every sound. She caught a glimpse of a gate-pillar as they swung into the drive so she knows she is home. There was a time when she did not expect to see her house ever again, and despite her agonies she is grateful to be back. The past twenty-four hours have confirmed all she ever thought about the locals. Dupont brought her to this backwater from the refined environment of her birthplace above Villefranche-sur-mer, where she was cosseted and pampered. Here there is nothing but yokels who destroy her confidence and turn her into a simpering bundle of shattered nerves. The courteous and aristocratic Hauptmann always brought an air of refinement into the house on his visits, and now this handsome major has rescued her, and brought her back to her husband.

She glances at Monique, but there is no change in the glassy eyes. She sits up painfully, clutching the bedding tightly about her. Her nerves are shattered, but she knows that once she is with her husband he will take the burden from her. She closes her mind to the bestialities that took place at the farm, shutting out the memory of those animals with their drooling, filthy mouths. She shudders and eases her fragile body over the back of the lorry until her bare feet are on the ground. A couple of Müller's soldiers spare her a glance as she treads painfully between the broken glass and sharp stones towards the door. Inside, the hall is a shambles. Everything that is breakable is smashed or torn apart. Instinctively she makes for the study.

The major is unprepared for the ear-piercing shriek when she sees her husband's body. He turns quickly to see her standing framed in the doorway, her face a grotesque mask with gaping mouth and horrified eyes beneath a wild tangle of frizzy hair. A trooper comes running to see what is wrong.

'Get her out of here!' shouts Müller. 'Take them both to the local doctor, or anywhere, as long as they are out of my sight.'

When they have gone he stares out of the window. There is something dangerous brewing in the village, he can feel it. Somewhere in the area those prisoners are still at large, and the airman may well be with them. It would be impossible for them to hide if they are not helped by the locals, yet the damned Hauptmann continues to treat them softly. It is time the SS took control completely. First the dissenters must be found and disposed of. In a small community like this they must be known, and it is only a matter of prising open a few talkative mouths. If the garrison troops are too soft to do what is required, then the battle-hardened SS will show them how it should be done. It must be quick and effective; something that will shock them out of their complacency.

'Herr Major.' The man stands rigidly at attention, mud-splattered and wearing goggles pushed up onto his helmet. He must be the despatch rider sent to find Becq.

'Well?'

'Sir, the Hauptmann's car has been sabotaged. It was blown up at the checkpoint by a booby-trap in the boot. Three men have been killed, including the driver, and several others are wounded, some badly. The Hauptmann escaped with a few minor cuts and burns.' He looks uncomfortable. 'I – I could not deliver your message, Herr Major. They are attending to the injured in the guardhouse and refused to speak to me.'

'Is he still at the guardhouse?'

'Yes, sir.'

Müller looks at the body and at the broken window. 'Find Oberfeldwebel Schöler. Tell him I want two Panthers brought down to the village with as many infantrymen as can be spared from the barracks. He is to rout out the inhabitants and separate them into two groups – males and females. The males will be taken to the square, and the females to the schoolhouse.'

'The children, sir?'

He looks hard at the messenger. 'Male and female, I said.'

'Yes, Herr Major.' The man's arm springs out in salute, and he turns to march out. The motor-cycle engine roars into life and fades away from the house. Today the village will learn the meaning of being a conquered race. He glances at the clock. Ten thirty: all should be ready by noon. If he looks to his left through the trees he can see the flag with its stark, black swastika hanging limp over the door of the Hauptmann's office. If only the Wehrmacht was not led by old-fashioned traditionalists like Becq it would not be necessary for the SS to be sent to prop up floundering units like this. The old guard with their Prussian ways and Junker traditions do not inspire the total dedication that SS officers do. Many look upon their Führer as merely a political leader rather than the personification of the new Germany. Müller had taken the oath when he joined the Schutzstaffel: 'I swear by God and this holy oath, that I will render to Adolf Hitler, Führer of the German Nation and people, Supreme Commander of the armed services, unconditional obedience. And I am ready as a brave soldier to risk my life at any time for this oath.' It allowed no modifications to suit changing circumstances. Hitler is the embodiment of the Third Reich, and for an officer to falter in any way when carrying out his commands is unforgivable. When Müller joined the SS only men with the purest Aryan blood were admitted to the élite force, and to have as much as a tooth missing could jeopardise a man's chances of joining. Now it has been seen fit to allow less perfect specimens to enlist in the ranks; even foreigners, but even they are dedicated, and if all the forces of Germany had such devotion there would not have been the setbacks to the cause that have occurred. Today it is the turn of the major to remind the Wehrmacht that this is total war, with no room for sentimentality.

*

Malloy has no plan when he takes advantage of the disruption to slip away while the others run towards the gully. He heads straight back to the orchards with no thought other than an immediate desire to put as much distance between himself and that bunch of nut-cases with their crazy scheme as he can. It is Malloy first, second and all the way as far as he is concerned. The past months have dashed away any remote vestiges of patriotism he might have had, and all he knows is that he has been compromised all the way by a lot of idiots who are chasing round like amateur commandos with a bone-headed Frenchman.

He is tired and uncomfortable. The parts of his clothing that have managed to dry out are stiff with salt and his body stinks with sweat and grime. They could have been on their way to a POW concentration camp where there would be hot grub and a nice safe spell sitting about doing nothing until the end of the war. That is what he should be entitled to in the circumstances, and these damn fools have thrown away any chance by going along with the Resistance. That bastard Mortimer has plagued him ever since the day they met in barracks, and it looks like there might be a way to get even with him.

Almost by accident he blunders into the garden of Dupont's house, creeping up the path towards the half-open door of the conservatory. There should be food, and possibly warm clothing inside, and from the rear the building seems deserted. Beyond the boundary wall he can hear the sound of traffic, and a motor-cycle suddenly coughs into life before roaring off down the drive towards the main road, causing him to duck into the shrubbery until the noise dies away. The doorway looks inviting from here, and he makes a quick dash across the path into the sultry warmth where the heady scecnt of plants and the hum of bees fill the atmosphere. Coloured glass panels cast blues and reds across the ordered array of pots, while a vine spreads its tentacles over the inside to mottle the walls with the shadows of its leaves. Still no sound, and the interior door leads straight into the dining-room, with yet another door opening directly to the kitchen.

There is an assortment of food to select from, and he grabs handfuls of bread, biscuits and cheese, stuffing everything into a linen sack that he finds hanging behind the door. Now he has enough to keep him going for some time, but there must be other things in the house he can use. He slips back into the dining-room and goes towards the door leading into the hall just as the handle turns. There is no chance to hide, and he is stranded in the centre of the carpet when two SS troopers walk in. Their reaction is spontaneous and he finds himself staring into the black barrels of two sub-machine guns, reaching frantically for the ceiling. One of them moves in quickly to run his hands over Malloy while his companion settles his gun to point at the AB's midriff. There is no emotion in the soldier's eyes, and no doubt that the trigger will be squeezed if he so much as blinks. When the search is complete they stand back and beckon with their guns towards the door. In a moment he is facing Müller in the study, and still Dupont stares at the telephone, waiting for someone to stretch him out before rigor mortis freezes him in a sitting position.

The trooper who searched him drags out his identity discs and hands them over to the major. Malloy is wearing enough uniform for Müller to recognise that he is a British sailor, and he sends for an interpreter before turning his back to stare out of the window. The old clock on the mantelpiece ticks the seconds away in solemn dignity while they wait, and the AB's mind is working overtime. He has been in situations like this many times, caught in compromising circumstances by the law, with the need to think quickly to wriggle out of desperate predicaments. Here he knows there is every chance of being shot, for he has seen faces like Müller's: handsome men with eyes that can knife into a man so that he knows there is no use trying to bluff or wheedle his way out. If he is to wriggle off the hook it will be on the officer's terms, and he will see through any smart tricks the AB is foolish enough to try. Men like Müller are no strangers to Malloy. They are always the ones who run the show, demand most respect and are the most feared amongst the criminal fraternity. Malloy has Müller taped as though he has known him a lifetime, and knowing is understanding. He can see light at the end of the tunnel now, and has no doubt about what he must do as soon as the interrogation starts.

The interpreter is one of the Hauptmann's clerks with rimless glasses and a nervous tick. He is alarmed at being summoned by the SS and quakes in front of the major. He nods like a nervous hen when Müller speaks, then turns to Malloy: his face filled with anxiety. 'The major wishes to know how you came here, and where are your comrades?'

The AB glances towards Müller, and for the first time their eyes meet. The major sees something in the prisoner's eyes that makes him wary as Malloy responds in a voice tinged with insolence. 'Tell yer boss I 'ave run away from the others because I don't like what they're doin'. I ain't part of their set-up at all, and I only want ter do what's right by 'im.'

The clerk looks bewildered for a moment before the implications behind Malloy's words dawn on him. The major listens while he studies the AB. There is a mixture of interest and contempt on his face, but deep down he knows he can trust what the sailor tells him because he is an unscrupulous rogue, with one thing in mind: to save his own skin. The quandary is: how far will he go? Even the most infamous villain baulks at the prospect of shopping his own mates. Yet there is something in his manner that suggests he has an axe to grind. Müller goes to the door and barks an order. Two troopers enter and carry away the body of the conseiller. The major waits patiently while the mess on the desk is cleaned up, then takes his place at the desk to sit looking up at Malloy's crafty features. They both know in that instance that they are in tune, and the information pours out of the AB's mouth as fast as Müller can formulate the questions. The interpreter's expression grows more and more amazed as the AB goes out of his way to offer traitorous information to the smiling major. It confirms everything he suspected: there are villagers, many prominent ones too by the sound of it, who are plotting and acting against the occupation forces. The AB doesn't know their names, but he can identify them.

Müller would have liked to capture the small band of saboteurs red-handed at the radar station, especially after they have walked through the Hauptmann's so-called security net, but that would be going too far. A telephone call will put Becq in the picture, then it will be up to him to apprehend the raiders before they can do any real harm. Even the Wehrmacht should not be able to bungle such a simple operation. Müller has a more important task. He is convinced more than ever that the village is rife with back-stabbers and agents for the Resistance. He will root them out and set the whole village an example they will never forget. Even now Schöler's Panthers are on their way, and the major has the scenario all worked out in his mind.

The telephone rings harshly and he lifts the receiver. It is Hauptmann Becq, but before he can launch into his monologue of outrage Müller stops him, making him hold the line while the two guards remove Malloy. The interpreter is told to remain in the room next to the study, and only when he is totally alone does Müller allow Becq to go on. With set features he listens to the Hauptmann's tirade: waiting for the initial outburst to subside before interrupting with some questions of his own which Becq answers tersely. Yes, he has sent a squad to capture the Britishers. No, he is not hurt badly.

Yes, security has been tightened, but he will register a strong protest to his headquarters over the way Müller has over-ridden his authority by taking some of his infantry from the barracks without so much as a by-your-leave. Also there should have been liaison before the Panthers were removed from their positions, for he had arranged his defences with them in mind. They were ranged on a 'fixed line' to cover the road from the headland, and now there is a gap which he is unable to cover with his own guns. He would like to know if the tanks are to be returned, or should he re-arrange his whole position once more.

Müller almost simpers into the telephone. 'You can dismiss any idea of an invasion here, Herr Hauptmann. My prisoner says the hopfields of Kent and the secluded estates are full of men and equipment. All closely guarded and ready to move. Every day his family at Sevenoaks have to wait long periods just to cross the road while hundreds of military vehicles pass by in convoy. It all points to an invasion on the Pas-de-Calais, as I have always said. Anyway, look at the weather. Only an idiot would expect an invasion force to sail in gales like this. No, Herr Hauptmann, the enemy we must combat is here in our midst. A more insidious one, Becq, and a far greater menace to us than a fictitious landing.

Becq remains unconvinced, and insists that the infantrymen be returned to their duties forthwith. He must be able to maintain his defences at full state of readiness. Müller's reply is blunt and insulting, and the Hauptmann smashes his fist on the desktop with a shout of rage. He has no wish to go screaming to his superiors, but they must know if there is a weakness in the West Wall, and it requires someone in higher authority to deal with the major, so the Wehrmacht can get on with the job. But that is easier said than done, for communications are disrupted.

In desperation Becq contacts Müller's own superiors, but the 21st Panzer Division HQ is reluctant to become involved in what they consider to be a local wrangle. They are used to Wehrmacht officers becoming hysterical when they are shaken out of their complacency by the SS, and they are much too busy consolidating their position fifty kilometres back from the coast, for there are signals coming in of wide-scale bombing of coastal defences, and rumours of paratroop landings. No one really expects an armada to come in these atrocious weather conditions, but there is an air of nervous anticipation everywhere. A petty squabble in a remote Normandy village holds a very low priority.

The villagers hear the tanks approaching from the headland long before the muzzle of the first 75mm appears round the corner of the end house. The Panther looks massive with its wide tracks grinding into the street as it leads its companion into the village to stop with motors throbbing ominously near the square. Behind them come the infantry marching in single file down each side of the street until they are lined up along the edge of the pavement. Leutnant Schöler sits beside the driver of a motor-cycle combination as it drives between the ranks to pull up in front of Müller. He alights and stands for a moment to make sure every man is in position before he salutes the major and reports all ready.

Müller responds to his salute. 'Get everyone out of their houses, Leutnant. Have one of your Panthers ranged at each end of the street facing this way, and I want sentries posted to prevent people leaving or entering. If anyone tries to make a break for it, shoot him down. I want everybody in the centre of the village. No one is to remain inside under any pretext. Understand?'

It is the SS troopers who enter the homes and chase the occupants out into the street while the Wehrmacht line the sidewalk watching the bewildered inhabitants swarm into a milling throng between them. Mothers clutch babies while children hang on to their skirts. Old men with cigarette ash spilling down their black waistcoats gaze about them in squint-eyed confusion. Farmers caught away from their small-holdings clutch sacks, thinking their wives will never believe this excuse for returning late from the village. Even the sick are routed out of their beds and forced to join the crowd.

Now the troopers move in to separate the sexes. Boys are dragged from their mothers and ranged with the fathers, brothers and uncles beneath the tall elms, while females are herded into the school-house. Etienne is the senior man now that Dupont is dead, and eyes are turning to him as he stands amongst the men. He attempts to speak to Müller, but a sentry slaps a rifle across his chest to stop him. Eventually the shuffling subsides and there are only the plaintive cries of children, and the mournful wail of the wind through the eaves of the old houses.

A stray, black dog lollops into the street, its lean body twisted into all manner of contortion by the violent wagging of its tail, for the scene delights it as it bounces from one pair of polished boots to another while the blank-faced men ignore it. Just one man moves and the dog's eyes gleam when Müller strides down towards the square. It scampers after him until he turns to glare at it. The black body slides to the ground, crouching with its tail flicking uncertainly. The eyes lift hopefully for a moment before the head is turned away and it slinks off with an occasional nervous glance over its shoulder. Müller takes his stance in front of the males, savouring their anxiety, watching to see which ones avert their faces.

'Choose a couple of representatives,' he says quietly, 'and make sure they speak German. I will see them in the Hauptmann's office in five minutes. Do not keep me waiting.' He turns about smartly and marches briskly across the street.

Three minutes later Etienne Martin and the doctor walk in to find the major seated behind the desk. The room is gloomy despite the big window. Schöler stands behind Müller, and two fully armed sentries are positioned with their backs to the wall behind them. Etienne peers about and gasps involuntarily when he sees one of the British seamen between two more sentries. It is the sullen one who had little to say when the plans were made in the study.

'You both speak German?' asks Müller.

'I speak it,' replies the doctor. 'Monsieur Martin is our senior village elder now Monsieur Dupont is dead. It is right that he should be here. I will interpret.'

Müller slams his hand hard on the desk. 'You damned French!' he barks. 'Can you not obey one simple order?' He rises from the desk to come round and face them. 'You have betrayed our trust. The Hauptmann has been lenient, keeping restrictions to a minimum, even though the village is near the coast and in a military area, and this goodwill has been repaid by treachery and deceit. Today I am going to root out the corrupt influences, Herr Doktor. One way or another I will find the dissidents and clean up the village once and for all.' He peers at Etienne. 'It is up to you now. The task can be completed peacefully, or it can be done the hard way, whereby guilty and innocent suffer. The onus is on you.'

While this is interpreted to Etienne, Becq's little clerk comes across to Müller. He has had a whispered conversation with Malloy and now he nods towards Etienne as he stands rigidly at attention talking into Müller's ear in brief, staccato phrases while the major's face remains impassive. When he is finished Müller nods curtly. 'Well, Herr Doktor. It seems this pillar of local society you bring with you is the ideal person to solve the problem.' He goes back to his chair, the anger melting from his face to be replaced by a look of satisfaction as he looks directly at Etienne's twitching features. 'Tell your esteemed elder he has five minutes to get his thoughts in order. Afterwards he will have a choice. Either we can go out together and he can point out all his friends in the local Resistance, or he can watch his neighbours punished en masse.' He looks at the shocked expression on the doctor's face and grins. 'Oh, I too am surprised, Herr Doktor. Who would have thought such a puny replica of a man could be a rebel?' His grin fades. 'Five minutes to make up his mind. The alternative sits waiting at each end of the street, for if I do not get what I am after every male person will be stretched out in the gutter and my Panthers will crush the life out of their verminous bodies. It will be up to Monsieur Martin how many of his friends are to die, and to ensure that everyone knows who bears the responsiblity for their deaths he will stand in front of the school with the women watching from the windows.' He rises from his chair, nods for Schöler to follow, and goes to the door, where he turns to look at Etienne. *'Cinq minutes, monsieur. Comprenez-vouz?'*

Eight

Morale in the tiny hut is at a low ebb. The wind batters the corrugated iron with relentless fury, and its sound adds to the general feeling of dejection. The big dish aerial can be easily seen through the numerous peepholes, mocking them as it probes the sky with its antenna, but more important to the watchers is the constant lookout kept from the small, steel platform built behind the control cabin. The whole unit swivels on top of a concrete base, and Mort's guess is that the guts of the thing is in the base, while the displays and instruments are in the control-cabin. As far as he can make out there are only three men manning the station, but it is in full view of the range-finder and several small anti-aircraft installations dotted about the area. The Colonel is absolutely right when he says it would be madness to venture out into that bare landscape in daylight. Yet in the back of everyone's mind the mental picture of Malloy telling the Germans exactly where they are and what they are about destroys whatever confidence they might have.

'This,' says Envoldsen with profound conviction, 'is fuckin' stupid!' He eases his frame into a more comfortable position as the others look up in surprise. No one has spoken for twenty minutes while they wait, listening to every sound, and watching every movement.

'What are you saying?' asks Potter.

The PO's face is blunt and serious. He is not used to arguing with officers. Gunnery Instructors teach, and are taught to jump first and ask questions afterwards. 'We all know Malloy will do anyfin' ter clear 'is yardarm, sir. In next ter no time this 'eadland is gonna be swarmin' wiv Jerry pongoes, and they will know exactly where ter start lookin'. We are playin' silly buggers waitin' 'ere, and the longer we wait, the worse it is gonna get.'

Potter looks uneasy. His own enthusiasm has wilted considerably since they left the house. It would most surely have been suicide to surrender after becoming involved with the partisans, but this adventure – and that is what it has become – is way out of their league. 'We can't keep changing our plans,' he says weakly.

'Plans!' scoffs Envoldsen. 'Wiv all due respect, sir. What bloody plans? This is a job fer a bunch of well-trained commandos. We ain't even dressed fer it. I'm sorry, sir, but you are a pilot, and although yer might be a wizard at flyin', I've spent months at Whale Island learnin' the rudiments of this sort of thing, and I know it ain't on.'

Potter looks from one to the other, seeing their eyes focused on him, and knowing full well that they have more respect for the seaman PO than for him. He is from another world, just one step up from the RAF in their eyes. 'Are you suggesting we give up, PO?'

'What I'm sayin', sir, is that a good leader knows when it is time ter give up on a scheme that's gorn sour.'

The Colonel steps in. 'I too say we should think again.'

'*Comment?*' Nicole has been listening suspiciously to the exchanges and though she cannot understand a word their faces tell her that an important new decision is in the offing. The Colonel explains briefly, and she launches into a tirade that sets him back on his heels until she finishes. His face flushes violent red as he dismisses what she is saying with contempt, but she will not be put down, and Potter becomes alarmed at their raised voices and steps in between them.

'What the hell are they on about?' asks Mort.

'It was too fast for me,' says Potter, 'but I gather she wants to get on with it, and says we talk too much.'

The Colonel shrugs his shoulders. 'I warned you that she is crazy, and very dangerous. She wants us to lead the Germans away while she does the job on her own.' He lifts both hands in despair. '*Mon Dieu!*'

'I see.' Potter's level tone says it all; he too has no faith in her, but Mort has been watching, and sees the blazing light in her eyes. Something about her sends a thrill through his body. She reminds him of a picture in an old schoolbook of a tigress defending her young cubs. He is heartily sick of the way things are degenerating. All the big talk at the start has given way to a stream of limp excuses. He rises to his feet.

'She's bloody right! We have pissed about for long enough. If you lot creep off back the way we came you might be able to get to the mainland; after all, they are watching for people trying to get in, not out. The Colonel's got some explosives. Blow something up on the way, even if it is only a gorse-bush, to take their minds off us for a bit. I've been watching that aerial. It takes twenty seconds to rotate, and for twelve of those seconds the platform is out of sight. There's a big clump of gorse half-way between us and the station. I reckon we could make the whole journey in two goes. Once we get to it the sentry can't see us, because the platform overlaps the base, and they've put up some wooden scaffolding on one side for some reason. If you can create a diversion, and keep them running round in circles for five minutes I am sure we can do the job.'

'You said "we"?' queries Potter.

Mort looks at Nicole. 'That's right, sir. The girl and me. I want someone with me who ain't gonna be thinking of saving his own neck all the time, and she's got fire in her belly, that one.'

'I'll go wiv yer, Mort.' Wordsley's eyes brim with hope.

'No, mate. Three's a crowd on a job like this.' He turns back to Potter. 'We ain't got a lot of time, sir. If Malloy's already got to the Germans, no diversion is gonna work.'

'I'm with a bunch of flamin' lunatics!' exclaims Wally.

'All right,' agrees Potter. 'Give it a go. You had better explain to the girl, Colonel.'

If Mort expected a show of friendship or appreciation from Nicole he is sadly disappointed, for when she hears what the

Colonel has to say she looks at the leading hand with an expression that says quite plainly, 'It is up to you whether you come or not. I don't give a damn either way.'

The others creep out along the path while Mort studies the terrain between them and the radar station. The wind buffets the hut, howling mournfully across the barren heath. He hopes the Colonel made it clear to Nicole that he is in charge, and that she is there to keep lookout while he tries to knock out the set. He glances at her as she stares out of her spyhole. If it were not for the hard set to her jaw, and the calculating coldness in her eyes she would be quite cute with her turned-up nose and full mouth. He senses she knows he is looking at her, but she remains in profile as the minutes go slowly by. The explosion when it comes is close enough to startle them. It shakes the hut and draws their eyes in the direction of the range-finder even as another blast reverberates across the plateau and a cloud of dust and smoke lifts over the dome.

'*Allez! Allez!*' A hand tugs at his sleeve and he follows her out of the door, crouching low as they race for the tower. She has either forgotten or chosen to ignore all their carefully laid plans, for she runs straight past the gorse-bush as though it doesn't exist. The man on the platform is totally absorbed in the explosions, and they cross the seventy-five metres without being seen. No need to worry about the language barrier he reckons. Apparently she is not going to do as she is told anyway. He is beginning to think the Colonel had her weighed up correctly. He hurls his body in close to the concrete and works his way round to the scaffolding. She has beaten him to it. Creeping through the timbers with her Mauser cocked ready while she gazes up through the trestlework.

He feels a thrill of alarm as he realises she is out to kill Germans, and his part of the exercise comes a very poor second. He catches up with her, grabbing her arm to swing her round facing him, with her back against the concrete. He grips the gun with his free hand, and jerks it down to the horizontal while he shakes his head violently at her. She stares back defiantly and attempts to wrench the gun away, but he holds it tightly, pressing her against the tower until she calms. When he is sure she is calmed down, and most of the excitement has left her eyes he eases his grip, placing one finger warningly over his mouth to quieten her even more. Her body loses its tenseness, and he is able to let go of her, placing both palms flat down in a gesture that says quite clearly, 'Take it easy.' Reluctantly she nods, and when he beckons her to fall in behind him she does so without taking her eyes off him. With one final look to make certain that she is under control he creeps forward again, searching for an opening. They can hear the hum of electrics from a vent just above their heads. He points and tugs at one ear, and she nods understanding.

A rattle of automatic fire snarls from the direction of the range-finder and there are excited shouts from above them, but they close their minds to what might be taking place, feeling their way round the cold base until they reach a steel door that stands slightly ajar. Now they must move with infinite caution. In *Cyclops* the unit was inside a cage, with the switches and dials outside, so that no one came into contact with the high voltage equipment. Apart from routine inspections and maintainance by the artificers, it was left unmanned for most of the time, for these are the internal organs of the monster needing only to be exposed when they malfunction. Nevertheless they have been lucky so far with that mad, undisciplined dash across the open ground. It was a miracle they were not spotted, and he goes cold at the thought.

A cough freezes them both, and they flatten even more tightly against the wall. There it is again: a dry, racking cough from someone who is used to coughing as a matter of course. Mort can see part of the opening, and whoever made that sound is just inside, probably looking out to see what all the fuss is about. Again it comes: the harsh, dry, old man's cough. Another explosion, followed by erratic firing, and a white-coated figure comes into view, peering short-sightedly through rimless glasses. He is a grey-haired man with a white moustache bristling beneath a bulbous nose. Mort has seen dozens of this type about the workings of the radar equipment, especially when it has been newly installed. They even go to sea from time to time, giving advice to the artificers, and making special adjustments when necessary to get the set working properly. They are the 'maker's men', jealously nursing their expensive product as it is taken over by the new operators. Boffins, aloof from what goes on about them for much of the time, and totally absorbed in their specialised vocations.

He feels Nicole moving out from behind him, and before he realises what she is about she smashes the butt of her automatic into the man's skull. He goes down without a sound with blood oozing from a stark gash in his shiny, bald pate. Shaken out of his reverie he helps her drag the limp body into the gloom of the interior, where they push the heavy door shut behind them. It will take more than a few bullets to penetrate the concrete or the steel door. Now to see what the layout is, and if indeed it resembles anything he is used to.

There is a cage all right, not unlike the ones he has seen, and inside several valves glow with pulsating energy. One of those valves is a very expensive one called a thyratron and must be treated with great respect. If switches are closed out of sequence, or without the correct time-lags it will blow, with devastating effect. At the end of a short passage a panel of switches and dials is attached to the wall, and, glory be! notations in red with what must be time lags alongside the rotating switches. Now he must think. There in one corner is the big master switch with its twin arms clamped firmly into the terminals, glowing dull copper in the vague light. He has always had a sadistic desire to wrench one of these big switches out of its sockets and enjoy the fireworks when he thrusts it back again to send a huge surge of unbridled power through the shocked, delicate components. This is like a boyhood dream come true.

Outside the noise has ceased and an ominous silence hangs over everything. He hardly dares to think about what the others might be facing, but in his imagination he puts himself inside the cabin above his head as he pulls down on the heavy switch. Surprisingly the lights stay on and they can hear the rotating mechanism working. So this isolates the throbbing heart of the set only. In the cabin the operators will see their displays die and look at each other, thinking that the boffin is down here, probably messing about with the electronics, for there has been no explosion, nor any sign of activity in their vicinity, so why should they associate the shut-down with the goings-on at the range-finder?

He allows twenty seconds or so to elapse before he slams the lever back into its contacts, and the response is far more spectacular than he could ever have imagined. In fact, it sends both of them cringing to the floor in one corner as vivid blue flashes dazzle their eyes, accompanied by sharp cracks like the sound of whip-lashes. While arcs of violent electrical discharge leap from one valve to another with the acrid stench of burning rubber.

Boots ring on the metal ladder outside and Mort clasps his hand down on Nicole's gun as she prepares to blast away at anyone who enters. For a moment they are safe behind the thick concrete walls, and the steel door can only be opened from the inside. Someone bangs on it with a solid object, shouting:

'*Onkel Willi! Onkel Willi! Welche Beschwerde haben sie?*'

Mort places his hand over her mouth as they look at Uncle Willi's prone figure stretched across the passage, content to allow the poor old scientist to take all the blame for the failure. But this place is getting to feel more and more like a dungeon to the leading hand.

*

Hauptmann Becq has recovered from his ordeal at the barrier, and a squad of his infantrymen have brought in the British seamen, along with a badly wounded Frenchman who was captured while making a suicidal attack on the range-finder. He looks at his watch, smiling. It is only half an hour since Müller's message, and already he has the culprits under guard. Even the exalted SS could not have done much better. He takes some pleasure in telephoning the major to say the prisoners are on their way, and suggests holding back any further action to root out the local Resistance until they arrive, so that an identity parade can be arranged. He is sure that one or two of the seamen will co-operate if they are offered leniency.

He has just replaced the receiver when a report comes in to say there is a malfunction on the Würzburg. It sounds as though that old goat of a scientist locked himself inside when he heard the explosions and has either electrocuted himself or blown himself up. They cannot open the door, and the small ventilation grill does not allow them to see into the smoke-filled chamber. The old man is probably dead, or soon will be, for the place is full of poisonous fumes.

He sends an urgent call for engineers with cutting equipment. It is the Navy's machine, so he can leave it to them to get it functioning again while he attends to more important things. If he doesn't get down to the village quickly, who knows what that hot-headed Nazi fanatic will do?

*

When Müller gets the news it leaves him in a quandary. Outside the melodramatics are being played out like a Wagnerian saga and he will look a complete idiot if he calls it off now. The tension he has so carefully built up in the street will evaporate and they will be faced once again with defiant villagers banding closer together with renewed courage. He decides on a compromise. He lines the Frenchmen up and drags Malloy out to walk slowly along, picking out anyone he can recognise. No one will be allowed back into their homes until the British prisoners have been brought back from the headland, and he refuses all requests for special concessions for the sick and elderly. Whatever happens he intends to have a final confrontation with the inhabitants, to root out the cancer once and for all. If necessary it can wait until dawn, after they have had an uncomfortable night to think it over.

To Malloy it is utter confusion. He understands only part of what is going on as he is led out of the office. When he moves down the ranks of villagers hostile faces stare back at him. He recalls Etienne all right; who could mistake that little bumpkin? But the others make no impression at all. After he has progressed down half of the line with no result Müller becomes impatient, venting his spleen on the unfortunate interpreter who relays the major's displeasure with a warning in his tone, and the AB realises that his future is on the line again: unless he can come up with a few results.

In true Malloy tradition he decides to use his imagination, and dismayed innocents suddenly find themselves hauled out of line when the accusing finger is pointed at them. By the time Hauptmann Becq arrives there is a bedraggled group of protesting inhabitants milling about his headquarters, and even Müller has doubts when Etienne admits his own guilt, but declares that most, if not all, of Malloy's selections are totally guiltless. The whole thing is turning into a farce. The tanks have stopped their engines, but remain like prehistoric monsters with their long snouts threatening the empty street. The women are demanding nourishment for screaming infants in the school, while bored adolescents become fractious and quarrel with each other. The men who have not been accused are taken to a small granary and made to sit on the floor while SS guards patrol the loft above their heads, and a heavy MG 34 is trained through the open doorway.

Becq doesn't mince words when he sees the full extent of Müller's fiasco. Rank is forgotten as he voices his outrage. This has been his village, and his responsibility throughout the occupation. Now it is a disorganised rabble, and the co-operation he has so painstakingly built up between himself and the leaders of the community has been destroyed by Müller's stupidity. Now, with the increased threat of invasion, men and equipment which should be deployed on the headland are here, standing guard over a bemused gathering of local farmers, businessmen and others who have enough to contend with without becoming involved with bands of hot-heads who roam the countryside. Did the major really expect anyone to believe that his tanks would deliberately crush innocent people?

Müller's face is infused. 'Do you think otherwise?' he yells. 'I will do anything to rid us of the scourge that threatens our war effort. The order still stands, Herr Hauptmann. I will give them one more night to consider, and if they do not produce the full list of dissidents by the morning there will be reprisals.' His face takes on a look of contempt. 'I will withdraw my Panthers, however, since they offend your finer instincts. But remember, Herr Hauptmann, it is your men who will be stabbed in the back.' He walks out of the room, thrusting aside a despatch rider who comes in with an urgent message for Becq.

In the distance flares illuminate the underside of clouds, and a sound like the continuous roll of distant thunder weighs heavy in the air, while the ground seems to vibrate with the concussion of massive detonations. The atmosphere is charged with pent-up energy as Müller's men watch him stride along, their eyes shadowed under the rims of their helmets. Now and again someone looks up as a new sound comes, but the sky remains clear, although the drone of aircraft hangs like a canopy over the whole area.

Becq reads the signal and feels a nervous thrill pass through his body. All along the coast the Allies are bombing coastal defences with blockbuster bombs. Airfields are under constant attack, and every bridge on the Seine has been destroyed. There are rumours of paratroop landings, and reports of Resistance activity everywhere. He gathers up his gear before going out into the street to rap out an order, and the infantry are marched away from their positions to go back to barracks, leaving the SS to watch over the desolation of the village. The wind still blusters through the houses. Surely no invasion fleet will sail in this! Yet even the village cats and dogs cower into corners, as though they too can sense some new, frightful event that is about to happen.

As he is driven out towards the headland, he remembers the radar unit and becomes concerned. Although the Kriegsmarine is responsible for the giant set, it is his own weapons that must react when targets are located, and the two biggest of these he has named himself: Fasolt and Fafner, after the two Wagnerian giants. Their 22cm barrels can hurl missiles 22,000 metres out into the Channel, and they are but two of many situated strategically along the coast. They need early warning and precise ranges and bearings to perform well. So it is imperative that the big Würzburg is brought into action as quickly as possible.

In the command post there is an air of tension. The men watching the instruments do so with their shoulders and necks taut – they will suffer for that later, he thinks abstractly. They too can hear the growing rumble lifting and falling with the wind. He responds to the salute of Hauptfeldwebel Kraft, the battery sergeant major, who keeps his four corporals on their toes with constant reminders of their doubtful parentage. 'Leutnant Fuchser has gone to the radar station, sir. The Navy is to bring up oxyacetylene equipment to burn through the door. There has been no response from the old man, and they think him dead.'

'Very well. Do they know how long it will take?'

'No, sir.'

Becq nods. No need for him to start ranting and raving at them, they know full well how important it is to get their task completed. Despite the humid warmth of the bunker he shivers. Against all reason the Hauptmann knows that things will never be the same after tonight, and as though to confirm his thoughts the strident blare of the alarm klaxon sears his brain with its chilling cry.

While it is still sounding the anti-aircraft guns add their thumps and chatter to the chorus, pock-marking the sky with bursting flak as tracer arcs towards a swarm of diving Marauder bombers swooping out of the cloud. Peering through the observation slit he sees the first pair homing in on the radar installation. There must be at least nine aircraft coming in from all directions to plaster the whole headland with their bombs and shooting at everything that moves. Reports begin to come in from anti-aircraft gun positions telling of weapons put out of action and heavy casualties amongst the crews as they crawl desperately away from their posts to find holes in which to hide from the murderous attack. The truck with the oxyacetylene gear is hit and destroyed on the road near the barrier.

The American aircraft have the sky to themselves, for Göring's Luftwaffe is nowhere to be seen.

Another shape in the sky catches his eye, a lone Mosquito reconnaissance aircraft flying steadily above the carnage, heading straight inland along the line of the Caen road, taking it directly over the village.

*

In their concrete cell Nicole and Mort hear the klaxon, followed immediately by shouts from the men outside, and the crunch of heavy boots. The nearest gun opens up with a sudden burst as they hear the howl of aircraft, and the ground shakes with the blast of exploding bombs. Mort taps Nicole on her shoulder and indicates that they must get out while all is chaos. She nods, and they move towards the door. As he reaches for the top bolt he is thrown back by a violent explosion, and the world splits wide open as a thousand coloured lights dance in front of his eyes. His mouth chokes on dry, acrid dust, and he is on his knees, groping amongst the debris, unable to hear or feel anything.

Gradually a grey light penetrates the thick veil of dust and he can see the jagged edges of the doorway gaping open, with the heavy door wrenched inwards, hanging on one twisted hinge. His head is filled with a whirlpool of sound. He hears himself groaning and coughing while he strives to pull himself upright. His whole body shakes, yet he can feel no pain, just a terrible weight bearing down on him and turning his legs to jelly. All he can do is heave his torso out of the rubble into the vague light beyond. His brain is beginning to function, and he can hear the sour note of another diving aircraft. It sends him scrambling for cover against the concrete base as the shadow of the 'plane sweeps across him. He screams as more ear-shattering blasts tear at his brain, and a falling mass of burning wreckage crashes to the ground just beyond the base. He grovels into the hard-packed earth, moulding his frame into the foundations while the world rocks and pulsates.

He hardly feels the grip of her fingers when she takes his arm to wrench him up. Her hair hangs limp across her blackened face and she looks wild and savage in the half-light, like some primitive beast in the midst of the dust and smoke. She is urging him to respond, pulling at him to follow her, hoping he is recovered enough to struggle with her. He had taken the full force of the door as it burst in on them, and for a moment she thought he must be dead, then, miraculously his prone body rose up, a grey, shapeless figure with blood soaking into the thick grime on his face.

She was shaken by the blast, and could not move her body at all for a while, as though every nerve had ceased to function. Yet her brain was fully aware of everything. The appalling din bore down on her, driving into her head like a hammer while she gasped for air and prayed for strength to return. She watched him haul his limp body out of the door, dragging it through the dirt with both legs stretched out slack behind him. She heaved while her tortured lungs ached. They felt as though they had collapsed and would never inflate again. The second blast shook the chamber, causing a large piece of electrical equipment to crash down inside the cage, and a chunk of concrete fell from the ceiling, bringing a mass of rubble with it. She catches her breath at last, taking in big gulps of air as her legs begin to function, groping her way through the door until she finds him lying inert against the wall.

Together they push up from the rubble, until he is on his knees and his head is clearing. The raucous crashing and bellowing of the air-raid revolves about them like a cacophony from hell. He forces himself up onto his feet, leaning heavily against her small frame. She has all the strength as they stagger along across the heather with a pall of smoke following to cloak them as they go. Past the gorse-bush and on to find that the tin hut is no more, the rusty old galvanised iron sheets have been shaken to pieces and thrown in all directions. They are

entirely dependent on each other as they push towards the
gully where they fall to the cool ground at the bottom of this
sheltered haven while the tumult boils above them. It is like a
piece of sacred earth, undefiled amid the crashing wilderness
on every side and they huddle close together in its cradle while
their shattered bodies recuperate.

The sound stops as quickly as it began. For a while a silence
settles over them while their numbed ears recover, and the
wind brings men's voices from beyond the ridges of their
haven. Colours are fading as the short summer night closes in,
but just to lie there close together is enough, for the sounds are
like a dream. Voices, wind, the distant noise of an engine and
the brave chirping of a bird; they all add to the tranquillity.
When full darkness comes they will have to move on, but for
now there is time to rest.

Mort wakes first with the cold night sweeping into his back.
His mind is fully alert, crystal clear, as he waits for his ears to
tune to the sounds about them. Nicole's body is pressed
against him, and he can feel her warmth through their clothes.
The night is black and filled with noise, and there is a strange
quality to it, as though it is charged with menace. There is the
grumble of distant gunfire and the constant drone of aircraft,
like a vast, never-ending migration of war-birds, filling the sky
from horizon to horizon in long skeins, all heading towards the
east. There are other sounds too, much closer. Ominous,
metallic noises mixed with men's guttural voices.

He pulls away from her and cautiously worms his way up the
side of the gully until he can see over the edge. The night is
alive with light and sound. Towards Caen he can see flares like
translucent fireballs floating gently down on their parachutes.
The echoing whoomp of anti-aircraft guns is thrown back
from the sky; a portentous, sinister growling that seems to
come from the rim of the world. It is as though they are in the
centre of a great black bowl and the grotesque melody of war
threatens to pour in over the brim.

Close by shadowy figures move about and stentorian
commands startle the darkness. The headland seethes with

suppressed agitation. The world is holding its breath, waiting for a colossal happening. Nicole comes up beside him and they stare out into the night and he knows she senses it too. There will be no moving out of their hiding place while every eye watches, fully alert, and sensitive fingers itch on trigger-guards. They are held spellbound by it all. Without knowing they hold hands while they watch the panoramic spectacle grow from the fringes of their small world. They seem to be the only living beings to witness the coming of the storm.

'*C'est l'invasion, n'est ce pas?*' Nicole breathes, and Mort can feel the excitement within her.

'Yes,' he replies, grinning. 'The invasion is here.'

*

Müller is becoming more and more concerned. He had seen the Mosquito fly over the village, knowing full well that its cameras were clicking away, and that his two Panthers were in plain sight. There is an eerie glow in the sky and the night is alive with a growing menace. Yet headquarters insist there is no threat of a full-scale landing in his area, despite the continuous procession of aircraft passing overhead, and the rampant rumours that circulate of paratroop landings near the city. The buildings seem to crowd in on him as he walks down the street towards the bridge where the two Panthers glint in a flickering yellow light. The crews are bunched together between them, for no one sleeps tonight, and he can feel their eyes follow him as he turns back up the street.

What the Hauptmann said is true, he can see that now. His tanks had been deployed carefully across the headland to back up the Wehrmacht, and these two in particular were ranged on the section of road leading from the headland so that their 75s could take care of anything the Allies tried to bring down that single artery. What if headquarters have got it wrong and they do land here? What will be their first major objective? It had to be Caen, and he has left the door wide open for them. Becq will not have time to re-deploy his guns. He was relying on Müller's tanks to seal the gap, and rightly so. More and more the picture forms in his mind, and for the first time in his career the SS major feels the awesome weight of real anxiety welling up inside. He would have condemned any other man for acting the way he has done. His SS are skulking in the village while the Wehrmacht man the defences as they should. He feels physically sick. The moment he gives the order to move out everyone will know he is admitting he has been unprofessional, and for an SS officer that is unforgivable.

Back in Becq's office Müller stands for a moment staring at the wall-map, visualising the dragon teeth on the beaches, the lines of posts driven into the sand with their explosive charges waiting to rip out the hulls of landing-craft, the gun muzzles poised over the cliffs, and the scores of binoculars staring out into the blackness of the ocean for the first sign of an approaching armada, and then his eyes focus on the blatant gap where his tanks should be and he almost sobs at his own stupidity.

To Schöler standing near the desk, the major seems to have diminished in size as he peers at the map as though he has not seen it before. The three other men in the office are staring too and the Leutnant barks at them; driving them back to their duties as he comes round the desk to stand at Müller's side. The silence is embarrassing, but he knows enough to refrain from intruding on the major's thoughts.

Suddenly, as though a glimpse of Schöler's uniform from the corner of his eye triggers something in his brain, Müller snaps out of it, pulling himself upright as his jaw squares and the arrogant gleam comes back into his eyes.

'Schöler,' he says, still looking at the wall-map, 'at first light I want the tanks driven back to their positions alongside the road,' He swings round to face the Leutnant. 'You will remain here with a squad of men. When Hauptmann Becq's men bring in their prisoners they are to be taken with Monsieur Martin to the square in front of the school-house, put against the wall, and shot.'

Schöler looks down on his boots for a moment. 'Are they not to be questioned, sir?'

Müller smiles pityingly. 'Are you serious? After the fiasco with our so-called informer? He lied through his teeth, Schöler. Is there any doubt that the others will do the same? Now I have seen them all lined up I do not believe there is one amongst them who has the guts to be a partisan, but they will think hard before they defy us in future. As soon as you have completed the executions you can release the remainder.'

Schöler snaps his heels. 'Yes, Herr Major.'

'Good. Now I will have a little talk with our Englishman. Send the interpreter in and leave us alone.'

Malloy is sat with his hands spread out on a bare, wooden table, watched over by one SS guard. His face is full of confidence when Müller enters to stand in front of him with an evil twist to his mouth. They remain staring at each other for a long while as the AB's confidence drains and he begins to look anxious. He switches his gaze to the interpreter.

'What's up for Gawd's sake! Aint' I done enough fer 'im?'

Müller smiles thinly and replies with a sharp sentence. 'You have lied to me,' he accuses.

Malloy's protests are interrupted in midflow when Müller pulls his Luger from its holster and takes deliberate aim at the horrified face of his captive, allows a few seconds to elapse while he savours the abject terror in the AB's eyes, then pulls the trigger. A neat hole appears in Malloy's cheek, and the back of his head splatters against the wall.

*

The women have re-arranged the desks and furnishings to allow space on the classroom floor for everyone to stretch out. No one sleeps, however, for a strange, sulphurous light fills the sky above the black silhouette of the house opposite the big window. There are no blackouts, so the strange glow filters in to illuminate their faces with a ghostly light as they huddle in small, amorphous groups while mothers suckle babies, or try to comfort hungry children as they listen to the distant thunder. Those whose husbands or brothers have been identified by Malloy are numbed and shocked, refusing to be comforted by the others.

Throughout the long hours of the night nerves stretch to breaking point, and some look for an easy prey on which to vent their anger. In one corner, remote from the other women, Madame Dupont nurses her distraught daughter. Her own body is a mass of agonising wounds, but her concern is for Monique as she stares into space with vacant eyes and clutches at her mother with shaking fingers. A half-circle of shadowy figures closes in around them, picking at their clothing with cruel talons, and dragging them out of their corner into the centre of the room. Madame Dupont utters a sharp cry and a hand clamps her mouth as she is wrenched away from Monique. There is an evil, stealthy menace in the way they go about it, for they do not wish to alert the guards, and as they scuffle a ball of plasticine is crammed into her mouth.

Simone Floquet is the ring-leader, wild-eyed and witch-like with her frenzied hair and blazing eyes. She is the mother of the twins, and they inherited their villainy from her, for she has an all-consuming corruption that alienates her from the villagers. The Germans have dragged her from the dark little hovel just outside the village, and now she is amongst them with her evil malice feeding on their fear. Her face is twisted with hate, and her eyes gleam in the yellow light as she spits out her spite.

'Well, Madame Dupont, with your airs and graces. What say you now that your friends have deserted you? Will you turn your head away tomorrow when they hang our menfolk as you did when they hanged the curé? Will you do your Lady Bountiful act when the job is done, patting widows on the head and saying how sorry you are, and how terrible it all is?'

She has attracted a small knot of women now, and they close round the two pathetic figures while she taunts them. Most of the others look on horrified as a few of her old friends join in the taunting. They are revolted by the venomous creatures who hurl vile accusations into the two white faces and fight for a space to hammer vicious blows at them. Skipping ropes are produced from a wall cupboard, and no one protests as the two victims are bound to chairs in the centre of the throng. Madame Dupont sobs wretchedly as a pair of blunt scissors scythes through her hair, cutting and hacking great swathes of grey tresses and hurling it in all directions with screams of triumph, goaded on by chanting women who are no longer concerned that their wild cries might be heard. There is something obscene in the way they go about their task, and when it comes to Monique's turn she remains unmoved and dull-eyed throughout. At last it is done.

Madame Martin moves into the hushed circle with her face set in an impassive mask as she releases the ropes to free both wretches with their bald, bleeding heads. 'Are you satisfied now?' she accuses. 'Are we no better than the Germans? Think of that when they hang our menfolk in the morning!'

They drift away into corners, ashamed to look at each other as the sounds grow outside the window. Beneath them the floor vibrates to a series of tremors as more explosions rock the foundations. A deep, rolling sound comes from the headland, more menacing than anything they have heard before, and the sky is lit by a far brighter glow, with flashes above the rooftops as the volume of sound increases. They look at each other with puzzled eyes, for there is something about this new sound that curdles the blood. In the street outside there is hardly any movement and only a few soldiers move about furtively. The tanks have gone too. When the door is cautiously opened the corridor is empty, with the big, double doors at the end swinging in the wind.

'There are no sentries!' exclaims a choked voice. 'Most of the troops have gone; the street is almost deserted.'

They rise and file out into the corridor and on through the doors into the street. The first grey light of a new dawn is turning the houses to beige, and they can hear a massive bombardment rumbling from the headland. The SS take no notice of them as they spread out in all directions while the first of the men comes creeping out of the granary, testing the air with his eyes and ears. Moving figures wander aimlessly about, hardly knowing which way to go. Some search for their kin while others run towards their homes, and the village feels strangely quiet without the grey-uniformed patrols. Madame

Martin stares towards the granary as the men come out in ones and twos. Etienne is on his own, gazing about bemused until he sees her looking at him and goes towards her with his peculiar waddle. The explosions are continuous now, and pieces of tile are being shaken from the roofs into the street, while the monotonous drone of aircraft fills the sky as they stand together in the centre of the village, listening to the convulsions coming from the sea.

'Etienne!' she says at last, 'it has come – the invasion has come!'

He says nothing, looking up at the sky with his face orange in the dawn. A truck rumbles down the centre of the street, wandering from side to side as though the driver is uncertain of what he sees, and wary of the dark buildings with their black openings. It pulls up at the Hauptmann's office and two guards drop over the tailboard to stare about them while their sergeant gets out of the front seat, and with his rifle gripped tightly in his hands moves to the door. Major Müller looks up as he enters: 'I have the British prisoners, Herr Major.'

Müller rises from his chair. 'How many men have you?'

'Just myself and two others, sir.'

'Find Oberfeldwebel Schöler. Tell him the prisoners are here and the executions must take place immediately. I will take your truck. You and your men will assist in the executions.' He stumps out before the sergeant can reply.

*

Hiding in the school toilets Camille knows nothing of this. She has seen the two Dupont women shaved and knows she will be next when they find her. She is trembling and sobbing heavily while she loosens the velvet belt from her waist and passes it over the cross-beam. The toilet is no more than a row of holes in the ground, but they are quite deep enough for her purpose as she knots the belt tightly on her neck and drops her legs through.

Nine

Able Seaman Knowles – 'Know all' to those who are familiar with his ways – watches the spectral shape of the huge battleship emerge from the deep gloom, to glide past the landing-craft as though they are standing still. Turning to the young Canadian leaning over the rail of the gun platform beside him, he remarks with a disdainful sniff, 'They must 'ave drogged 'er out of 'er safe berth with a bloody 'urricane 'awser. Spends all their time swingin' round bouys those big, useless bastards. Aground on their own empty milk tins most of 'em.'

He says it all with an air of great authority, for Knowles has been in the Navy twelve years and no one ever suggested that he should consider promotion. He is a hard man to impress, and even the great cavalcade of assault craft fails to stir him as the huge armada assembles for the biggest invasion of all time. Five thousand vessels of all types creep through the night, rolling and pitching to the lively sea with their bellies full of men and machinery of war. Their bilges reek with vomit as the flat-bottomed crafts bucket their way across the Channel, and the young soldier had staggered up out of the foetid stink of it all to fill his lungs with cool, fresh air, hoping to drive away the nausea.

He had hoped to be alone for a while, so that he could nurse the growing anxiety that threatens to break his resolution. As his companions succumbed to the misery of their sea-sickness he had found it increasingly difficult to bury his fear, and their distress only added to it. So he sought out this corner where he could lean out and peer into the shadows at the reality of the moving ships, trying to drive out the vivid pictures his imagination painted in his mind of what lay in store when the ramp went down in the morning and he found himself running out onto that alien beach into the teeth of a grey enemy who waited behind a wall of concrete to rip his body apart.

The sight of the great ship towering into the sky with her big guns trained fore and aft sends a surge of confidence through him. She is majestic as she heaves her ponderous bows clear of the swell with wraiths of spray sweeping aft across her fore-deck. The deep blackness had opened for a moment as though someone had swept a veil aside to give him a sign and lift his spirit, and it did more to restore his courage than any platitudes from hard-nosed sergeants or glib-tongued officers.

Now this Job's comforter has ranged alongside him with his morbid words and sombre portent of doom and gloom. 'Obsolete, those bastards,' states his tormentor with an air of profound knowledge. 'Won't last five minutes against an air attack.'

Together they watch her disappear into the blackness, and the night closes in once more, so that they seem to be alone in their little tin box of a ship with its vulnerable open hold, thick with the sound and stink of vomiting soldiers.

The 'Big Useless Bastard' has steamed south from Greenock to join the invasion fleet. In an ideal world she would be obsolete, for she is older than most of her crew, and saw action with their fathers at the Battle of Jutland, but the niggardly budget of pre-war Britain had decided to revive her ageing bones and bring her back into the Fleet, rather than spend out on a modern battleship, when everyone knew there would never be another war. Since then she has given good account of herself in different theatres of a modern war, and men who knew her spoke of Narvik, Calabria, Cape Matapan and the surrender of an Italian fleet who found her and her colleagues more than enough to handle.

Now the Big Useless Bastard is at first state of readiness as she steams towards the Normandy coast to fulfil a duty for which she is most suited. True, only six of her eight fifteen-inch guns are serviceable, and she has a temporary patch under her boiler-room bilges, but her high velocity shells will penetrate the thick concrete emplacements that defy the efforts of a thousand bombs dropped by the Allied air forces as they saturate the coast from a great height. Men like the young Canadian will bless her guns when they see the bunkers pulverised until they are impotent, while the dazed occupants stagger out with their heads whirling with the nightmarish percussion of her giant shells.

Before dawn the first projectiles leave their bins far below in the magazines. Each is loaded into its hoisting cage with four silk-clad quarter charges of cordite, then raised to the working chamber beneath the gun. Under the practised control of the operator the shell and charges are thrust into the gun-loading cage to be taken up to the gun itself, where they are rammed into the gaping breech before it is slammed shut.

'Left gun ready! Right gun ready!' reports the man on the breeches, and the gun-layer and trainer line up their pointers with the indicators from the directors mounted high on the superstructure.

'Layer on! – Trainer on!' and the firing circuits close to light the 'gun-ready' lamps in the director.

At five-thirty a.m. on the sixth of June 1944 the first broadside roars out with a deafening blast that fills the mountings with acrid smoke. Drill, drill and more drill has turned the gunners into machines as they shake their heads clear of the stunning shock of their own guns. While the first six shells lift into the atmosphere to arc over and fall towards the distant targets the second charges are being loaded. Within a minute the gun-ready lamps are glowing once more in the director. The double gong sounds a warning to the gun-crew and the muzzles belch flame again. Six more projectiles are on their way, each weighing almost 2,000 pounds. The Big Useless Bastard sits in her position eleven miles west of Le Havre and methodically pulverises the German defences in her sector.

*

After the initial excitement dies down, Mort and Nicole retreat into their gully to lie listening to the mounting percussions of the distant conflict. The whole headland seethes with activity as the Hauptmann's men close up to their action stations, where they man their posts with growing tension. They are safe for the moment in their gully, for no one comes closer than twenty yards, but soon dawn will be here with its revealing light and Mort knows it is imperative that they be well away from here before then. An anti-aircraft gun nearby opens up with an earsplitting chatter as though to emphasize his feelings, but one cautious look over the rim of their hide-out is enough to show there is no chance of a quick dash to the mainland. The sentries manning the barriers are fully alert, while inside both pill-boxes their colleagues watch the surrounding area for the slightest movement. Mort slumps back. For the moment at least there is nothing they can do but wait.

The first bomb bursts with an all-consuming blast that rocks the earth and shatters their ears. Before they can recover another sends them cringing into a tangle of arms and legs in the depths of their refuge, where they lie quivering as the high-level attack goes on. The awesome noise destroys all thought while the ground lifts under their bodies with each new detonation. The atmosphere stinks with the acrid stench of explosives, and Becq's men can do little more than cower at their guns, praying for the nightmare to pass. It seems impossible that anything can survive the terrible holocaust as tons of bombs saturate the landscape, blasting the few distorted pines to denude their branches, leaving the blackened, skeletal remains stark against the tortured sky. A mass of gorse is set alight, and the eager, blustering wind rushes in to join the fun, fanning the flames so that they spread across the heath, rooting out the men at the light anti-aircraft guns and exploding their ammunition. A pall of evil-smelling smoke drifts inland from the coast, and because the concussion of the bombs has made a vacuum it hangs in the sky above them while the air is sucked out of their bodies. It is like trying to breathe in a bag as they huddle into mindless balls, trying to shut out the madness while the erupting filth falls in on them.

When it ceases the Hauptmann can take stock of his situation and take heart when he discovers that his bunkers have withstood the bombing. There are many casualties amongst the AA gunners and other men who have been caught on open ground, but all the main defences remain intact and Fasolt and Fafner still poke their aggressive snouts out of their massive emplacements to sniff the wind coming in from the Atlantic. Most damage is to morale, especially amongst the younger men who have never been under fire before. The unbelievable din has scoured their minds to leave them bewildered and bemused, so the older, battle-weary men must take charge, chiding and threatening them back to their duty. They recover to take their stations as binoculars peer out into the vague morning light and see targets growing out of the west like a steel tidal-wave, stretching across the horizon as far as the eye can see.

The morning mist rolls back to unveil the full might of the advancing armada, and it is a sight that takes an icy grip on the stoutest heart of the most hoary campaigner. When Becq sees it he has to catch his breath before he can deliver his orders. Nowhere in his wildest dreams could his imagination conjure a nightmarish vision like this. It is as though the whole world is moving against them. He is about to order the controllers to select their targets when the first broadside of six fifteen-inch shells shrieks out of the sky and bursts on the cliffs. The shock of the combined impact is like an earthquake, and before he has time to recover a second broadside tears the air apart. At one minute intervals the high-velocity shells thunder in to find their marks. Concrete is no match for them. Armour-piercing projectiles bury their hardened noses into the reinforced bunkers and detonate amongst the crews inside. Time and time again, at just over one minute intervals, the broadsides come, blasting steel, concrete and minds with their methodical carnage.

Mort lifts his head when the bombing stops. Smoke and dust are pouring into their gully, choking their lungs and burning their eyes. He looks up into the billowing mass of gaseous fumes that permeates across the entire span of the isthmus. It is now or never he realises, and while the guards are still numbed by the bombs and this ready-made smoke-screen hides their movements they must make a dash for it, and get across the neck of the headland before the Germans recover.

He pulls at Nicole's sleeve, nodding his head towards the surface. She is black-faced and vague, but she responds, and he can see a light in her eyes as she allows him to lead her out of the gully, and they creep across no-man's-land until they find the hiding place where they first hid with the Colonel, Potter and the others a thousand years ago.

*

Potter and his small band of disconsolate seamen are on their last legs as they wait in a bedraggled group, guarded by SS troopers, while the village simmers like a cauldron. The Colonel's plan had misfired from the start even though they had tried to follow his instructions to the letter, making their break when they heard the first grenade explode. Before they had gone thirty yards they were surrounded by infantry and taken into custody while the intrepid Colonel died in his futile attack on the range-finger. Now they are left to ponder over their future as shouts and scurrying boots show how jumpy the Germans are as the sky erupts with mysterious lights and flashes.

'I don't like the look of it, sir,' remarks Envoldsen, sotto voce. 'There is somethin' cold and calculatin' abaht these blokes. They're not like the squaddies that captured us on the 'eadland. They even smell like soldiers.'

'Yes, PO. I know exactly what you mean. I'll see what I can do.' He approaches the nearest sentry, indicating the two and a half stripes on his shoulder-straps. 'Officer,' he says slowly, trying to recall the few bits of German he learned while on holiday. 'Officer, *komme, bitte.*' It is a pathetic effort and the man just stares back blank-faced, then waves his sub-machine gun to send Potter back to his place.

'You will not speak to the guard,' Schöler's voice comes from the door. 'You will not speak at all. Your right to be treated as prisoners of war ended when you joined with the partisans.' He raps out an order in German to the guards. 'I have told them to shoot the next man who utters a word. Do not be impatient. We will not keep you waiting long.'

'He looks like an ordinary bloke under his peaked cap,' thinks Wally. Pale-faced and gaunt, the classic features of an undertaker.

There are more orders, this time from an NCO, and a sentry moves amongst them with a clasp-knife, cutting the strings of their dog-tags and putting them into his pocket. Potter's protest is cut short by a jab in his stomach with a rifle-butt, and a real fear begins to grip them as they realise how vulnerable they are. It is as though their identities have been stripped away with the little brown discs. They are lined up and the troopers bind their wrists securely behind them. Tiredness is forgotten now. The cold, efficient way their guards go about their business leaves them numb. There is no room for doubt now. Outside the light is growing, and with it the ominous grumble of conflict. More orders come, and they are prodded into movement by the guards who urge them out into the street, where a few villagers gaze curiously for a moment before moving on quickly about their affairs.

It is all very matter-of-fact, an incongruous charade while the pyrotechnics revolve about them. An open truck with canvas stretched across the back to receive their bodies. The blank wall that might have been designed for such an event, and the machine-gun set up on its tripod mounting with the gunner sitting high-kneed, holding the handles of the breech.

'Jesus Christ!' exclaims Envoldsen, and there is a strange sound from Wordsley, but they do not falter as they are marched to their positions and made to stand facing the wall.

'Barbarian!' shouts Potter. 'At least allow us time for a prayer!'

There is no response. The Leutnant checks their bonds and orders his men away, out of the line of fire. A choked sob comes from Wordsley. 'Jesus Christ!' repeats Envoldsen, his face slack as he takes it all in. 'I never thought I'd go out like this.'

With everyone in place Schöler takes one more glance round to ensure all is in order, then turns to move over to his own position. There, coming towards him with Etienne in the lead, is a scattered group of villagers. They are walking in silence, staring straight at the Leutnant as they move in to place themselves between the prisoners and the machine-gun. In vain the sentries shout at them and threaten them with their rifles, but the solemn procession continues and the crowd begins to thicken in the square. Now the women come to join their men, and they press right in until some are only inches away from the muzzle. Schöler fires his Luger into the air while his men rattle their bolts. It makes no difference. No one moves, even when he sticks the barrel into Etienne's stomach. ' '*Raus!*' he barks. ' '*Raus!* '*Raus!*' and incredibly they still do not move. There are too many for his troopers to move forcibly. Müller has left him barely enough men to carry out the execution. If he orders the gunner to fire it will be like mowing a field of wheat, and the massacre of almost the entire population of a village is more than even the SS can stomach with the sounds of an invasion coming from the coast, and in any case it would take a prolonged period of sustained fire to scythe through this mass of bodies. He has but one choice left. He yells at his troopers and two guards seize Etienne and haul him out of the crowd. Schöler points his Luger at the Frenchmen's head.

'Ten seconds!' he warns in French. 'You have ten seconds to move away.'

No one moves. The dull, peasant faces are blank and Etienne stares straight ahead as though he is resolved to die. Schöler has no orders concerning the civil population, and Müller has already backed down from the execution of the Frenchman, while everybody has been let out of the school as the emergency grows. Now the major and his tanks have gone, leaving his Leutnant in command. If there is an atrocity here today Schöler wants no part of it, for he knows where the blame will fall, and every minute brings more ominous rumbles from the coast. It is stalemate, far beyond the resonsibility of a mere Oberfeldwebel. He stands his men back in semi-circle with their weapons trained on the silent mob, and the machine-gun is set up on the back of the truck to command a better coverage of the crowd. A messenger is sent off to find Müller and tell him what is happening in the village. Meanwhile Etienne is taken away and put under guard in Becq's office while they wait for the major's orders.

Müller's world is disintegrating about his ears and with the coming of daylight the sounds of the invasion reach a new crescendo. All doubt is swept aside and he knows a full-scale landing is about to take place in his area. He should have moved his tanks under cover of darkness, but his obsession with the rebellious villagers dulled his senses to all else. Any idiot can see the mess he has made of things, and now he has to get the two Panthers back into position in case the Allies break out from the coast to begin their thrust towards Caen. Even now the ground beneath him convulses with the detonation of heavy bombs falling on the headland, and he can picture Becq in his command bunker trying to keep order amongst his troops while their minds are blasted by the awesome din.

To the major's tormented mind it seems the lumbering tanks are deliberately taking their time negotiating the houses and walls as they pick their way through to the orchards. The sky is throbbing with the roar of aircraft, and they will be vulnerable to any sharp-eyed airman who studies the uniform ranks of apple trees, but it is better than attempting to use the road. He raves at the tank crews for the timorous way they skirt the buildings, and urged on by his lashing tongue they plough through the masonry, demolishing walls as they grind their way through to break free of the village. They will find dubious shelter in the trees until they reach the fields that surround the clutch of farm buildings where they are to take up their positions once more to guard the road to Caen. He leaves them to press on while he swops his commandeered truck for the side-car of a motor-cycle combination and goes on ahead. They are to wait at the edge of the trees until he signals them to cross the open ground from his observation post in the loft of one of the outbuildings.

At that moment Schöler's messenger arrives to pour out the sorry details of his predicament in the village. He reels under Müller's violent verbal attack that sends him scurrying back with the major's reply. 'The Oberfeldwebel is to use his initiative and not come crawling to Müller with his problems. He is to shoot the bloody lot if he has to; for there are more important things going on at the coast.'

A heavy pall of smoke is drifting in from the headland. A thick, evil-smelling cloud that stinks of explosives and burning rubber. Trucks with red crosses emblazoned on their sides pick their way through a litter of wrecked vehicles and files of infantry, while medium shells whine overhead to burst on or near the road. Those shells must come from Allied ships, and he can imagine the turmoil taking place beyond the cliffs as invasion barges make their approach against the concrete defences. Everything seems to be in disorder and the trudging infantry look grey-faced beneath the rims of their helmets as they march in to take up their positions. Already several dead cattle lie belly-up in a field close to the road with their legs stuck in the air and insects already scurrying along their tongues into cavernous mouths. It is hard to believe that this beleaguered landscape is the same unspoiled countryside of yesterday. The deserted farm buildings look like a deserted oasis of stone amid the wasted fields that surround them. The walls are broken and choked with rubble where the Panthers thrust their ponderous metallic bodies into the rooms. Pathetic remains of domesticity show bleakly through the ruptured masonry, so that it is like looking into the decayed cavities of rotting teeth.

To one side there is a small, crumbling row of outhouses and pigsties before the farm gives way to empty fields that stretch out for a couple of hundred metres until they come up against the fringes of the orchards where his two Panthers should make their appearance at any moment now. He takes up position in one of the cowsheds, dismisses the combination rider and prepares to wait. His watch shows six o'clock, and the smoke is shredding now, stretching into drifting entrails across the pockmarked sky. In the distance small, buzzing insects swoop and soar against the pale sky and he realises he is watching an air attack taking place near the coast. They are too far away to concern him, and although the never-ending procession of aircraft dominates the morning, they are remote and offer no threat to him or his tanks.

He begins to feel better now. If all goes well in a few moments he will have his Panthers back into position with their 75s ranged on the road, and it will be as though nothing untoward has happened. There is a warm glow of confidence flooding into him, and he is almost looking forward to the sight of the first British tank rolling down the road towards his ambush.

*

Mort guides Nicole through a small lane with loose stone walls on either side. They are surrounded by movement and he stops at every gap to check before pressing on for a few more yards. She is moving with him now, no longer needing to be coaxed along as she recovers her senses. Soon she is keeping up on her own and even taking the lead at times as they move from broken wall to deserted building, dodging the scattered groups of soldiers, all the time staying close to the road that leads into the village. Mort is certain he will find the others there, or at least a place to hide until the Allies come. His limbs are aching with tiredness, and they are both ingrained with dust and filth.

Ahead he can see a group of farm buildings where it might be possible to pause for a moment, perhaps even find something to eat or drink. Although the place looks very deserted, he taps Nicole's shoulder and points. She nods agreement, and they creep forward together. There are squads of men moving in single file either side of the road, scattering into the fields to sprawl on the ground when low-flying aircraft zoom down on them. The Allied aircraft have the sky to themselves and are totally unopposed as they attack everything that moves. The only vehicles are those hulks that simmer with wreaths of acrid smoke rising from their wrecked frames.

Mort tests every yard as they go, but Nicole is showing signs of her impetuosity again now that she is fully recovered, and he has to pull her roughly to the ground as the roar of a motor-cycle engine bursts into life a few yards away. It revs several times before the combination, with only one rider, lurches out of the farm gate onto the road to race off towards the village. Gradually they lift their heads to find the scene unchanged, with the farm as still as death amid the outrageous bellowings of conflict.

'Come on!' he urges, taking hold of her arm, only to find it wrenched viciously away again. 'All right,' he grates into her belligerent face, 'have it your own way, you stupid bitch! We are in this together, gal, whether you like it or not, and you are not going to louse things up for me.'

She understands nothing of what he says, but he couldn't care less. He is beginning to get fed up with her attitude. After what they have been through together, and the way she helped him at the radar station, he would have thought the barrier would have broken down between them. But there is hostility in her eyes, and a determination not to be led. He cannot make out if it is him or men in general that she despises.

They are within the outer walls of the farm now, moving cautiously along the side of the pigsties that conceals them from anyone on the road, or in the farm itself. There is no need to hide the sounds they make, for they are overwhelmed by the uproar going on about them. They peer into the flag-stoned yard, and nothing moves. The secretive, grey-stoned walls challenge them with their covert, black interiors. Mort tenses to climb over the wall when a sound comes from inside one of the stables, sending them both diving for cover. There is a small gap between the loose stones through which it is possible to see into the yard, and as they watch an officer emerges, carrying a pair of binoculars.

'Müller!' breathes Nicole, so forcefully that Mort clamps his hand over her mouth and glares at her. The look in her eyes sets him back. She has never been less than hostile, but this look is one of pure malice. Her body is shaking with emotion and her breathing is laboured. He uses all his strength to hold her down, and only the noise of the invasion saves them from discovery. He waits with his hand clasped cruelly over her mouth, staring into her wild eyes, willing her to become calm. At last her body goes limp, and he is able to remove his hand from her mouth. He places his finger against his lips, jerking his head upwards. Her body still shudders, but her eyes have lost some of their wildness as she nods. Slowly, cautiously, he rises up until he can look through their spy-hole. Müller's back is turned to him as he peers up into the black orifice of a small, square hatch that opens into a hayloft. Mort nudges Nicole and gives a conspiratorial leer. She grins back, and her eyes light up as she pulls out a handgrenade from her blouse.

Together they watch while the major roots out a short ladder and climbs up into the loft. The moment he disappears she scrambles over the low wall, and Mort follows her into a dark, cavernous barn where the dusty remains of hay moulder amongst decrepit pieces of ancient farm machinery. Everything is highly combustible, and she rummages about silently in the dark until she finds an old oil-lamp, half-filled with paraffin, then she gathers anything else that will add to the blaze and roast the major alive in his confined observation post, and piles it up in the middle of the floor. Mort can only watch fascinated as she works beaver-like to build a stack of highly inflammable material. Not for her the straightforward blast of a grenade. She wants to see the major burn, and although her motives might be suspect, Mort realises it is far more certain than just tossing the grenade into the hatch. There is a sadistic pleasure in the way she goes about it all, and he has the impression that Müller is not the only man she would like to roast.

At last she is satisfied and backs out of the barn. Mort is left to his own devices, and she makes no attempt to warn him clear. It is as though he does not exist. If he is stupid enough to get himself burnt with the major it will not worry her at all. He takes away the ladder as a matter of course, then sets himself up behind the wall with his sten-gun trained on the open hatch. No professional soldier could have carried out the drill with cooler precision. She looks down at the British style grenade for a moment, weighing it in her hand while she judges the distance and her aim. Satisfied, she pulls the ring and releases the lever. The seconds tick by slowly for Mort as she waits for exactly the right moment to toss it into the barn, and Mort has to drag her down to take cover beside him or she would have stood there to savour the full effect of the blast.

Müller is thrown off his feet by the explosion. He had been searching about for something to smash through the roof so that he could see across the fields and signal his tanks. Now, empty-handed and half stunned, he scrambles aimlessly about in the smoke and the heat. The blast in the confined space is devastating, and in seconds the whole interior is ablaze, with flames searching out every aperture and seam in the floorboards, and when he looks towards the hatch he sees a solid mass of flame blocking his way out. Frantically he raises his boot and kicks at the rotting timbers and tiles, choking as the thick, billowing smoke engulfs him with its noxious fumes. He tears off his tunic, wrapping it round his helmet to cover his face while kicking blindly at the roof. He feels his boot go through and kicks again and again, hearing the tiles crashing down on to the flag-stones. The heat is intense. He knows his flesh is burning and yells profanities at the stubborn roof, lashing out wildly while the roasting flames surround him. In desperation he thrusts his hands through the gap, heaving, screaming, shouldering his way through the jagged gap; forcing his upper body further and further until it overbalances and he somersaults down onto the stone. Blindly he struggles to his feet, knowing he must get clear before the flames get to him. He thrusts out his arms with their charred, burning sleeves and staggers splay-legged into the blinding smoke until blessed daylight shows through for a second. He reaches towards it, tottering on rubber legs and croaking as he goes, a crazy scarecrow with arms waving frantically in a macabre dance right under the tracks of the on-coming Panther. The driver sees the blackened twisted features, white-eyed and insane for one split second before they disappear beneath his tank.

Cowering in their hide-out behind the wall, Mort and Nicole hear the screams and the roar of the tank as it climbs over the rubble into the yard. They can only lie still with their hearts pumping as they hear it stop, with its engine ticking over just on the other side of their wall. The snarling wail of diving aircraft sours the air as the Typhoons plunge out of the sky. They are the scourge of the Panthers, specialising in blasting the huge steel hulls wide open with their rockets, and here like a gift from heaven, are two juicy targets, naked and vulnerable, as if they were on exercise. The pilots aim their aircraft at the stranded tanks and carry out a precision attack, and in seconds both Panthers are blazing hulks, while Mort is running across the open fields with Nicole desperately trying to keep up. She is on her own now as far as he is concerned. He has seen enough of her to last a lifetime.

There are other shapes running through the fields, totally ignoring these two scruffy-looking peasants as they stream back to take up new defensive positions. Shells are falling near to the farm buildings, spurring them on towards the orchards, and all at once the futility of what they are doing hits Mort like a bombshell. No one could possibly recognise the filthy rags he is wearing as any sort of uniform, so as long as he stays with Nicole amid the general chaos they will pass for two distraught civilians seeking refuge from the conflict. He slows to a halt, holding Nicole back with him, until they stand panting in the middle of the field while infantry hurry past, weighed down with their equipment.

'The village!' he shouts at her. 'Where is the village?'

'*Là!*' she exclaims, pointing towards the east. '*Le village est là!*'

'Come on then,' he yells at her, grabbing her arm once more

and forcing her to walk with him at an easy pace while grey-clad figures detour round them; urged on by their NCOs as they scramble to take up a new line of defence. It is an uncanny experience, walking at a tangent through the retreating infantry as if they are invisible, in fact they suddenly find they are completely alone, walking into a vacuum as though they have strayed into hallowed ground where a swathe of unspoiled grass stretches before them, a void in one corner of the field where flowers grow and cattle graze aloof from all the turmoil. So abrupt and unexpected is it that they stop automatically to gaze about in apprehension. The violence rages all around, yet the rows of trees stand in silent ranks with their stark shadows staining the grassy lanes between them. Nervously they move forward, scrutinising the branches suspiciously as they go by until Mort stops. He can see the reason for all this solitude quite clearly, peering back at him from over the earthen bank that borders the orchard. Beneath the black skull and crossbones the legend *'Achtung Minen!'* screams its warning, and there are more of the same spaced out at intervals to the right and left of them; stretching away into the distance.

'Bloody hell!' he exclaims, looking at her as though she personally laid the minefield. 'Now what?'

She shrugs, looking to him for inspiration.

In despair he studies the area. Nothing will persuade him to go back amongst the infantry, yet there seems no alternative. He is about to retrace his steps when he notices the four cows chewing grass apathetically in the corner, eyeing the two intruders with baleful stares. They have had several hours to become immune to the abominable noises of war, and have found this small sanctuary where, if they huddle close together, they can tolerate the madness. Now they are being surveyed by two disreputable humans, and it gives them cause for a certain amount of nervous fidgeting.

'The cows!' he whispers harshly, picking up a long stick from the bank and waving it at the beasts. She looks bewildered for a moment, but soon gets the message and joins him in the round-up. The cattle stare back at them resentfully, and one big black one decides it is beneath her dignity to clamber over hedges, and lunges to one side in an effort to escape into the open field.

'Christ! There's always one!' gripes Mort as he runs at her with the stick brandished above his head. There is no grip in the bank and they are all fully matured, matronly bovines with an aversion to violent exercise, so, in the middle of a raging battle, with small-arms fire beginning to crackle close by, they engage in a tussle of wills with the lumbering cows. For a second or two Mort ponders over why the hell he doesn't just sit and wait for the outcome of the fight, and take his chances with whoever comes out on top, but there are too many unknown hazards in that, and he has no wish to be caught in no-man's-land between two trigger-happy forces who will consider all strangers a menace. No, farcical though it is, he can see no alternative but to use the cumbersome beasts as animated mine detectors, and get the girl back to the village, where hopefully, he will find his mates.

Sheer bloody-minded aggression forces the cattle over the bank with a great deal of stumping and bellowing as they manipulate their ungainly carcasses over the top with mini-avalanches of earth and stone cascading from their clumsy hooves until they regain their composure in the shade of the trees where the grass is rich and a cow can savour a more luscious meal. Life becomes more easy now, for the cows are quite willing to be coaxed along through this pleasant avenue, provided the pace does not exceed grazing speed.

One trick the Germans play is to set up bogus warning notices to confuse would-be invaders, and as they amble through the orchard Mort realises that this must be one such ruse, for they emerge unscathed at the other end with the roof-tops of the village in view. Leaving the cows to wander back amongst the trees, Mort and Nicole take the path leading round the small orchard that backs on to the Dupont garden, keeping low all the way until they reach the back of the house. It is completely deserted.

'Venez! Venez!' she insists, going in through the back door and beckoning him to follow her as she climbs the staircase to one of the front rooms that allows a view of the whole street.

It seems as though the whole population is in the square, with a few SS troopers standing on the edge of the crowd with their weapons held ready across their chests while a heavy machine-gun is trained out over the tailboard of a lorry. From this distance it looks as if the Germans have decided to murder the entire population.

Mort glances at Nicole to see for the first time emotion showing on her face other than belligerence. The villagers stand in a silent group, facing out towards their guards, it looks like a tableau from a Verdi opera. All that is needed is a deep sonorous chorus and the tolling of a death-knell to complete the scene. Her face is shocked, and her dark eyes filled with anguish as she stares hypnotically at the familiar faces, grey like stone under the peasant headware. He is moved to place a hand on her arm, feeling it tremble as she watches transfixed.

*

The bombardment has been going on for over two hours. At first the Big Useless Bastard had fired without spotter aircraft to direct her shots, but now her huge shells are falling with precision onto the defences. Twice she has shifted target, once to engage enemy ships in the Seine Estuary, then back to concentrate on the coastal batteries where the continuous pounding of her broadsides is blasting the defences to ruin, and destroying men's minds as they cower in their shelters. The first waves of landing-craft have already hit the beaches, and the time has come to shift target again.

'Signal, sir.' The midshipman is holding the pad under the captain's nose. It gives the co-ordinates for their next bombardment.

'What is it this time?' he asks the commander.

'A village, sir,' adding hastily when he sees the captain raise his eyebrows quizzically. 'It straddles the main road to Caen, sir. Reconnaissance photographs were taken by Mosquitos yesterday, showing no inhabitants other than Germans, and at least two large tanks deployed in the street. There can be no doubt that it is a strategic target, sir. Vital if our troops are to use the road for their advance on Caen.'

'Very well. Let's get on with it. Mustn't let the army down.'

'Shift target left – range 22,000 yards – target is a fortified village – all guns, with HE load load load.' The orders come through to the gunners, clipped and precise. The fifty-four foot barrels with their one hundred and eighty five miles of wire-rifling train and elevate to the new bearings, and the aircraft spotter watches for the first shell-bursts, so their aim can be adjusted to obliterate the sad little group of houses. The place still looks empty, although it is difficult to see if anyone is under the big trees in the square.

*

Schöler is furious when his messenger returns with Müller's ambiguous reply. The fighting is getting closer and he should be with his unit. He leaves a sergeant in charge and crosses over to the Hauptmann's office where Etienne is under guard, waiting to hear his fate.

'You speak any German?' asks Schöler gruffly.

'A little,' admits Etienne.

'Good. I have a compromise. Get your people back to their homes and the British will be treated as prisoners of war. You have my promise.'

'They will not believe you. They know the Allies are here. You will have no time to take prisoners.'

Schöler's facial muscles contract to contort his features with rage as he stares down at the bumptious little man, and his mouth tightens as he draws his Luger. 'Then we shall have to do it the other way, fat man. When we go outside you will tell your people to get to hell out of it or I will blow your head off, and if they do not move then I will shoot another and another until they obey. If anyone tries to make an aggressive move the machine-gun will mow the lot of them down. Do you under-stand?'

'It is too late for that now, Leutnant.' Becq's voice comes from the open door where he stands dishevelled and dirty. 'The headland is almost completely cut off. Two of your tanks have been destroyed, and the others are regrouping here.' He points at a spot on the wall-map. 'Go and join them, and leave this to me. If you leave by the bridge end of the street you will avoid running into the arms of the invaders.'

The SS officer swallows hard, chagrined at losing face in front of the Wehrmacht, but relieved at having the burden lifted from his shoulders. 'Major Müller ordered the prisoners shot, Herr Hauptmann.'

'Your major is no longer with us. It is my responsibility. Get back to your unit where you belong.'

Schöler snaps to attention and leaves with his men. Becq turns to Etienne. 'We have to clear the street, and there isn't much time. Tell your people the British prisoners will be treated according to the Geneva Convention.' When the little Frenchman hesitates he insists, 'Come, Monsieur Martin, I am not a fool. The way things are going I will be lucky not to be dead or captured by nightfall. For the sake of my men and myself I am not going to execute prisoners and invite reprisal.'

Etienne leads the way out into the street where Becq's infantry are setting up road-blocks in preparation for a street battle. A few, under the command of a sergeant, have relieved the SS guards and now stand facing the mob. No one pretends it is more than a token gesture, for the machine-gun no longer threatens, and the army is much more concerned with the growing menace from the west than a few restless civilians. The familiar figure of the Hauptmann and a few words from Etienne are all that is required to convince the villagers that their obligation to the British prisoners is ended. 'Go back to your homes quickly, and stay in your cellars. Do not venture out again until the fighting is over.'

From their window Mort and Nicole have watched the events unfold with growing bewilderment. She is hardly able to credit that there can be a reprieve for the villagers, yet as they watch Etienne addresses the crowd, and the SS troopers start to leave by the bridge road. Her hopes build up until tears course down her cheeks. They cannot hear what her father is saying, but they see the crowd breaking away from the square while Becq's soldiers back off to allow the villagers to stream out into the street.

No one obeys the order to return to their homes; they are much too excited and full of themselves for having made their stand against the oppressors and won through, and above all, the Allies are here. Liberation is only a few moments away, and they feel they have done their bit towards it. In vain Becq's soldiers yell at them, even threaten with their rifles, but the milling throng is fearless, incensed with joy and relief for coming through the test after facing up to Müller's SS, who had treated them with such contempt while they cringed in the schoolhouse and the granary, not knowing if they would live to see another day, let alone the end of the occupation.

The whole village is in chaos with children racing in and out of houses while their elders listen in groups to the advancing noises from the headland. Mort and Nicole race out to be amongst them and share the euphoria. She finds her father standing in front of their home with some of his friends, drinking calvados and laughing at the antics of the happy crowd. It is as though their joy has driven all reason from their minds, and it is Becq who comes to Etienne with a grave expression, forcing him to face the danger they are in if they do not get under cover before the fighting reaches the village, but the crowd is out of control, even if Etienne could be convinced, the population is spread throughout the village, and the Hauptmann suddenly realises that it would be futile to make a stand here, which would result in the slaughter of many civilians. There is one thing he can do for these people before he goes back to the fighting. He grips Etienne's shoulders, almost shaking him to make him listen and understand.

'Monsieur Martin. I am going to try to meet the British, and declare the village open to them. I will need you to come with me to convince them. If I succeed, you will be spared the consequences of a house to house battle: it will save many lives.'

Etienne's face sobers. 'I will come; but only if your men leave the village now, Hauptmann. Tell them to get out of our houses.'

For a moment Becq hesitates, then relents. There are positions to be manned beyond the houses, and he has few enough men left to man them. It is a small concession to make. They take a small scout-car to drive out on the west road, while his troops move out to their dug-outs and slit-trenches north of the village. Unbelievably, after the long years of occupation, the village is returned to the people, and for the first time only Normans walk the street. The first Tricolour flutters from Becq's office as a new sound comes. It is as though the sky is being ripped apart, and the ground convulses to a series of thundrous explosions just to the east of the village; stunning them all to silence while they stare at each other in disbelief.

*

'Down two hundred!' comes the order as the next six shells are rammed into the gaping breeches, and the gun-ready lamps light up again in the director. The double tone of the firing gongs sound in the turrets, and the guns recoil as six projectiles launch into the atmosphere in perfect trajectories to straddle the target.

'Spot on!' yells the excited spotter unprofessionally.

'Good shooting!' smiles the captain.

'Bloody well should be!' mutters the laconic gunner. 'This ship is geared to fire at targets that alter course and speed, from a ship that is also dodging and weaving. If we can't hit a stationary target from a static ship at a piddling ten mile range; we should join the army.'

So be it. No need to do more than carry out the drill, for broadside after broadside will soar away to land on the village as though the shells are travelling on rails.

*

The villagers still stand shocked and bemused when the second salvo arrives. Five tons of high explosive shells shriek out of the sky to erupt amongst the huddled buildings, blasting eardrums, heaving huge columns of smoke and flame high above the roof-tops, smashing every pane of glass, and throwing whole walls into the street. Enormous craters are torn out of the earth, and bodies hurled like rag-dolls across the smoking rubble, where they congeal in butchered chunks amongst the wreckage. Dazed people stagger about in the midst of it all, their minds emptied of reason, while others lie prone, burying their heads beneath their arms and sobbing into the dust as the blast rips at their clothing. Before the dust has time to settle, or the first screams rise above the noise of crashing masonry, the third broadside erupts like a volcano to drive hot wedges of agony into their tortured brains. The air is sucked out of the street as the hot blast tears through like a hurricane. People die without a mark on them. Others stare with vacant eyes at their shattered limbs or at lifeless bodies of loved ones. A woman stumbles along with a limp arm hanging in a shredded sleeve, and the stark, clean, white bone shows through her torn flesh, yet she makes no sound, just staggers blindly through the carnage; searching for oblivion.

Mort is thrown into a corner where he lies in a crumpled heap while the world goes mad about him. It feels as though his insides are blown apart, and when he tries to groan his tight throat clamps the sound in a dry grip as it struggles to gulp air into his deflated lungs. He can taste blood, but feels no pain. When he moves his limbs they seem to respond okay, and even his deafened brain has not entirely deserted him. He lifts his body until it is sitting up with his back against the wall, and when he forces his eyes open he looks out at a scene from hell, where demonic forces are tearing the guts out of the village and turning it into a nightmare of wreckage and grief. The sulphurous stench of explosives mixes with the acrid tang of dust and ruptured stone. The strident screams of the injured punctuate the pitiful groans and wailings that come from hidden corners where trapped and dying plead for light and succour.

From the depths of the carnage and suffering a few are rising to look about them with growing awareness, forcing reason back into their minds. They search round for others to join them in an effort to fight for life. An inborn will to survive lifts them out of the grime to battle on, and to help others to do the same. A driving force that has no reason, and thrusts aside self-preservation as they look to each other to bring sanity back to the village. Mort gets to his feet, joining other shapes as they go amongst the injured and the dying. He finds the doctor, white hair filled with brickdust and a fresh scar livid across his forehead, groping into the black depths of splintered timber to reach the soft arm of a weeping child where the flutter of a weak pulse sends him tearing desperately at the wreckage with his tender hands.

People are gathering at the granary, clearing away a passage to the wine cellar beneath the concrete floor. A chain-gang forms with no need of words of command or guidance, and they work in silent unison, passing chunks of brittle stone from the entrance. Already they learn to dive into holes whenever the shrieking comes, to wait until the ground ceases to convulse before carrying on with their task. Others are coming with make-shift stretchers, or just limp forms sagging between them. Mort coaxes the doctor away from his pile of rubble and the trapped child, for the pulse is no longer there, and the sobbing has stopped. He gathers his medical kit and swallows back the unprofessional surge of grief that threatens to consume him, and goes with Mort to the cellar where lines of broken bodies lie with blood oozing onto the cobbled floor.

They know the time-lag between each broadside now, and become adept at anticipating the next series of explosions, so that they are crouching in ready-made bomb shelters amongst the upheaval when the earth splits apart above their heads. Only those unlucky enough to be caught near the bursting shells feel the full effect. The bombardment seems destined to go on forever; until every last building is demolished, and the inhabitants buried beneath the rubble.

*

The spotter aircraft makes another pass over the village, but a huge pall of dust hides most of the street, and they see only the crumbling buildings. It has been a highly professional exercise, and there can be little fight left in anyone still surviving in that destruction. Already the advancing Allied troops are pouring across the fields on either side of the road, and it is time to call off the bombardment.

The news is greeted with smiles of satisfaction on board the Big Useless Bastard. 'Cease fire!' orders the captain. 'I imagine we have caused more than a few headaches there. Shift target right, we'll get on with our demolition work.'

*

They are fortunate with the granary, for it has tumbled sideways to collapse in an orderly fashion like a pack of cards, to lie across the strengthened roof of the cellar, giving added protection to those below. Mort teams up with Marcel, and they go out together on forays amongst the smoking ruins, seeking out the injured and bewildered. Some unfortunates sought shelter in cellars that have become death-traps, but while the bombardment continues they must wait, for it will take gangs of workmen to clear the wreckage and free them. An old man has to be forcibly removed from the ruins of his home, where he sits clutching a thin-necked bottle of calvados with a pear floating inside. He refuses to let go of it even when Mort half carries him to the granary, and hands him over to the doctor.

'It is old Norman tradition, *mon ami*,' he explains to Mort. 'It is for the marriage of the eldest son.' He settles the old man in one corner, leaving him to sit with his bottle in the midst of the bustle. 'I think this time there will be no marriage.'

'Mort!' Wally is fighting his way through the crowd with a

huge grin on his chubby face. 'Thank Christ I have found you. Potter says we are to stick together if we can.' He ducks as another broadside lands, rocking the cellar and showering them with thick dust, as a new chorus of screams comes from outside.

'Where are they?'

'Under the bridge with some French blokes and two German pongos who were supposed to be guarding us. They've decided to resign from the war. It's safe down there, Mort, 'ardly any shellin' at all.'

'You'd better get back there then,' grunts Mort as he sees Marcel looking at him. 'I'd rather stay here and keep busy.' He stares hard at Wally. 'It's our mob that's doing this, you know.' And without further ado he leaves the tubby seaman staring after him as he follows the Frenchman out again. There is a man digging frantically at an impossible pile of rubble, and when Marcel places a hand on his shoulder to pull him aside, he pleads with them both in a flood of words while his body shakes with uncontrollable sobs. Marcel kneels to place an ear to a small opening, and listens for a moment before motioning Mort to do the same. There are whimpering noises coming from below, and the unmistakable sound of running water. They exchange looks while the man waits; his face twisted with anxiety.

'Get some help,' says Mort, pushing at Marcel to make him understand before turning back to help the distraught man with his hopeless task.

Suddenly he stops to listen. At least two minutes have gone by since the last broadside, and a kind of numbed hush is settling over the village, as though an invisible sound barrier keeps the distant noise at bay. People are emerging from hidden places, rising up to stare about the wilderness of destruction that was once their homes. Marcel is returning with several men, and as he comes others join in a small procession until there are at least twenty volunteer diggers delving into the wreckage. Tools begin to appear. Pick-axes, shovels, and crowbars that eat at the small opening until it gapes open to reveal a small cavern where a woman lies dead, clutching a live, whimpering baby, while a dog cowers in a corner.

The water-level has risen so that the woman's face is submerged, and her hair spreads like a broken fan on the scummy surface, but the child rests with its head on her arm, clear of the water and Mort can reach down and gently pull it out through the opening. The father stares at it, and then at the seaman's face with eyes that cannot comprehend. Mort feels the baby wrenched out of his hands, and Nicole is there, looking at him with hate back in her face.

A new sound comes now. Growling engines revving as they struggle through the debris with steel tracks crunching into the broken stone. A sick feeling churns loose in his stomach as he stands with the small group of dirty people, staring into the thick smoke and dust towards the west as the shadowy shapes of the Sherman tanks rattle and roll through the devastation. They move aside in silence as the metallic monsters pass with shocked faces staring down from open turret hatches.

Infantry are coming down the street now, not even bothering to take more than token precautions, for they have been told this is an open village, and already Becq's surviving soldiers have been over-run as the Allies drive on towards Caen. The old man staggers out into the sunlight, still clutching his bottle. He fought his war thirty years ago, and is the only villager to raise a feeble cheer as the soldiers go by. He raises his bottle as though to toast them, only to see it snatched away by a grinning infantryman who smashes the neck against a wall and pours the contents into his mouth from a foot away, so that it runs down over his chin and onto his battledress. The old man screeches with rage and beats at the soldier with weak, skeletal hands until the angry Englishman wrenches him roughly away.

'Ungrateful Froggy bastard!' he yells at him, hurling the bottle to smash against a wall close to the old man's head. 'I've risked my fuckin' life ter liberate you lot, and this is all the thanks I get!'

If you have enjoyed this book and would like to receive details of other Walker Adventure titles, please write to:

Adventure Editor
Walker and Company
720 Fifth Avenue
New York, NY 10019